"You should marry someone to get the insurance you need."

Emma jumped up. "You want me to marry a complete stranger for medical insurance? This is ridiculous, Carter." She paced the length of the couch and back. "When I married Robbie, that was it. My one true love."

Of course, she was still in love with her husband. Understandable. "This would be a marriage of convenience only. Love wouldn't enter the equation."

"No, Carter, that won't work. You know I don't trust many people."

He hadn't given any thought to Emma's trust issues. He'd been more focused on coming up with a short list of candidates.

She set her drink on the side table and sank onto the couch, head in her hands. "If you didn't recommend marrying a complete stranger, it's not a bad idea," she mumbled.

Carter bit his tongue while he gave Emma time to mull over the proposal.

She faced him, perched on the edge of her seat. "Why do you think we should search for a complete stranger? Why not you?"

Heidi Main writes sweet inspirational romance novels set in small towns. Though she lives in central North Carolina's suburbs, she dreams of acreage and horseback riding, which is why her novels include wide-open ranches and horses. Before starting her writing career, Heidi worked with computers and taught Jazzercise. A perfect Saturday is lounging on the deck with her husband and watching the many birds in their backyard. Learn more about her books at heidimain.com.

Books by Heidi Main

Love Inspired

Triple C Ranch

A Nanny for the Rancher's Twins
A Family for the Orphans
Her Loyal Companion
The Farmer's Marriage Bargain

Visit the Author Profile page at LoveInspired.com.

THE FARMER'S MARRIAGE BARGAIN

HEIDI MAIN

If you purchased this book without a cover you should be aware that this book is stolen property. It was reported as "unsold and destroyed" to the publisher, and neither the author nor the publisher has received any payment for this "stripped book."

LOVE INSPIRED®
INSPIRATIONAL ROMANCE

ISBN-13: 978-1-335-90482-9

The Farmer's Marriage Bargain

Copyright © 2025 by Heidi Main

All rights reserved. No part of this book may be used or reproduced in any manner whatsoever without written permission.

Without limiting the author's and publisher's exclusive rights, any unauthorized use of this publication to train generative artificial intelligence (AI) technologies is expressly prohibited.

This is a work of fiction. Names, characters, places and incidents are either the product of the author's imagination or are used fictitiously. Any resemblance to actual persons, living or dead, businesses, companies, events or locales is entirely coincidental.

For questions and comments about the quality of this book, please contact us at CustomerService@Harlequin.com.

® is a trademark of Harlequin Enterprises ULC.

Love Inspired
22 Adelaide St. West, 41st Floor
Toronto, Ontario M5H 4E3, Canada
www.LoveInspired.com

Printed in U.S.A.

Every good gift and every perfect gift is from above,
and cometh down from the Father of lights,
with whom is no variableness, neither shadow of turning.
—*James* 1:17

To God be the glory.

Rich, I can't thank you enough
for your constant encouragement during this journey.
You truly are the best!

Shado, I never could have written a story
with goats in it without your help. I'm grateful
you allowed me to come to your goat farm twice and
most recently bottle-feed Adele—that was amazing!
This book is in honor of Shado's heart goat, Addie—
you will always be loved.

Chapter One

Emma Bailey sank into a camp chair outside her one-level rambler, exhausted yet thankful for the sound of laughter from her three-year-old triplets—especially Addie, whose recent illness had given Emma a terrifying scare. At least they now had a diagnosis of juvenile arthritis, and the treatment she'd been on for two months kept her out of pain. A bee darted toward Emma. She leaned back, tensing as it hovered near her pink top. When the insect flew away, she relaxed, but the chatter of her children playing in the yard brought back her financial dilemma. The biologics drug that relieved Addie's joint pain and swelling wasn't covered under their medical plan. Which meant every filled prescription plummeted Emma deeper into debt.

She lifted her head to allow the mid-June sun to heat her face. The magnitude of the past year weighed heavily on her shoulders. *Oh, Robbie, why did you leave me?* She never would have imagined her husband would die at twenty-nine, but brain cancer didn't discriminate. It had happened so quickly that she was still coming to terms with it all. Now she was left to parent their adorable children, alone. There were days she felt as though she wasn't up to the task. Then one of them would toddle up to her and give her a slobbery kiss.

"Mommy, watch." Mikey raced around the slide and threw his stomach on the belt swing, pushing off with his feet. Somehow, in the few minutes they'd been outside, he'd managed to get dirt smears on his chubby cheeks.

"Good job, kiddo." A few days ago, a friend from church had replaced their bucket swings, but the children hadn't figured out how to pump yet. Still, they enjoyed playing with the new attachments.

The goats bleated from their pens and Emma glanced over at her growing herd of close to thirty now. She held fond memories of her and Robbie taking this raw land six years ago and laboring side-by-side to turn it into a working farm. Her heart squeezed at what Jubilee Farm meant to her. And her children.

Addie screeched as she scrambled up the resin rock wall after Cassie, who wore a matching short and tee outfit. Their boisterous giggles warmed Emma's heart.

Her phone dinged with an incoming email. She pulled the device out of her back pocket and tapped on the mail icon. The last insurance company had finally replied! *Please, God, let this quote be an amount I can afford. I don't want to be forced to sell our farm.* She took in her happy triplets. *It wouldn't be fair for the children to lose the only home they've ever known.*

She had investigated every option to get the medicine Addie needed covered. This was her last hope.

She held her breath as she opened the email and scanned the text. When she saw the monthly premium was on par with the other outrageous quotes she'd received, her stomach dropped.

No. This wasn't happening.

The air whooshed out of her lungs.

She couldn't afford Addie's medication. With the debt from her hospital stay and the cost of the first two months of biologics prescriptions, their finances were precarious.

Emma pressed her eyes closed and dropped her head into her hands. Her body started to shake with shock. She could not, would not, fall apart, but she was fresh out of ideas.

"Mommy, you okay?" Her ever-compassionate Addie came over and awkwardly patted Emma's back, the motion she used as a mother to comfort one of the triplets when they were upset or having trouble sleeping.

She reached out and hugged Addie tight, hiccupping away the disappointment. Emma clung to her smallest child as though the embrace could somehow grant them the medical insurance they so desperately needed.

"What's going on?" She startled at Carter's voice.

He strode over, blocking the afternoon sun with his hand. His eyebrows were pinched together in concern, as if he could read her despair. He sported crisp dress pants and a striped polo shirt, all clean, which was more than she could say about herself. As an accountant, he always looked fresh and ready for a business meeting. Though, today his thick brown hair was messed up, as though he'd been running his fingers through it out of frustration.

Since she'd been focused on reading the all-important email, she hadn't heard his sedan pull into the gravel drive.

Before he could reach her, the triplets rushed at him, screaming, "Unkie C," their nickname for him, at the top of their lungs. He stopped to hug all three and asked how their day was going.

He'd been a part of the children's lives since the day they were born. If it wasn't for Carter McCaw, she wasn't sure where she and her precious bundle would be now. Her late husband's best friend was always there to stand in the gap for her. Offering to watch the children in the evening after she'd had a tough day. Or simply lending an ear when she needed to vent.

Telling Carter about the depressing email she'd just received made her stomach churn. He wouldn't believe it, but there was no way she'd tell him with six little ears listening. She'd have to wait until the children occupied themselves again at the jungle gym.

The sun shined brightly, the opposite of Emma's mood right now as Carter continued to give each of the triplets some attention. Her sweet goats must have spotted his arrival because they bleated from their pens to be noticed.

Once the children scrambled up the resin rock wall and settled in the shade of the covered fort, she pulled Carter to the far corner of the yard and told him the news.

His eyes widened and he shook his head, as though unable to comprehend the sky-high monthly premium.

"I don't get it. My plan includes the biologics medicine."

She snorted. "Carter, your firm has a gold-plated insurance plan."

He dragged his fingers through his thick brown hair that curled out at the base of his neck. "So you've contacted every insurance company?"

"All the ones that offer biologics in their plan." She twisted her fingertips in worry as the triplets played some imaginary game that made complete sense to them.

Carter wrapped her in a hug, which made her eyes tear. But she pushed the fragile emotions away. She was a strong, independent woman. Somehow, she'd figure this out.

Her husband's best friend had promised Robbie he'd be a fatherly influence to the triplets and watch over Emma, and for six months he'd done just that. Especially when Addie got sick and the coyote had become a threat to her goat herd. He'd actually stayed in their RV and taken care of the property for a week while she'd been consumed at the hospital with Addie and his mother had watched Mikey and Cassie. Emma drew in a deep breath, taking comfort in the clean, soapy smell of Carter before he released her.

The enormity of the situation grabbed her heart and squeezed, but she couldn't sit around and worry. She was a single mother with triplets. She had to make a plan.

But what?

"I've exhausted everything." She began pacing back and forth. *Think, think, think.* What other avenues hadn't she considered?

Carter touched her hand. She halted. "Wasn't the hospital social worker going to look into whether you qualified for state or federal help for this drug?"

"Yes. But there are none. At least not for this specialized drug." The sweet woman had been so compassionate. She'd even told Emma that other families were dealing with the same thing.

"You also contacted the drug company to see if Addie would qualify for their assistance program, right?"

"Yes, and I make too much to qualify." She gave Carter a wobbly smile. "I appreciate how hard Robbie worked while he was alive, but our survivor benefits prevent us from receiving aid, yet paying out of pocket for the medicine Addie needs will wipe us out."

He rubbed the back of his neck. "I wish I had that kind of spare money to loan you, but unfortunately, it's beyond my means. That medicine costs more than a monthly home mortgage."

She released a frustrated sigh. He was right. And paying for the drug would eventually bankrupt them. Then they'd risk forfeiting the farm she and Robbie had labored tirelessly for.

But this treatment made Addie feel like herself, and Emma would do anything to ensure the well-being of her children.

Addie came over to her, a slight limp in her right leg. Carter probably didn't even notice it, but as a mother, Emma sure did. She lifted her littlest and gave her a hug.

"You feeling okay, sweetie?" The doctor had told her that when she was active, it was normal to expect that Addie's joints might become slightly inflamed.

"Uh-huh, tired," she said as she rubbed her eyes with her knuckles.

Emma patted the back of her daughter's head, her silky-smooth hair soft on her fingers. The faint aroma of strawberry-scented kids' shampoo enveloped her.

To keep her daughter healthy, it seemed her only option was to sell this idyllic farm where she and Robbie had determined to raise their children. The place she housed her chickens and goat herd. This past spring she'd sold eighteen registered baby goats—or kids. Her gaze landed on her cute little family store that Robbie had built for her where she sold goat milk and fresh eggs daily, along with commissioned goods: grass-fed beef from a local cattle rancher, quilts, bead bracelets and earrings from a group of older ladies, and jarred relishes, jams and pickles from a local farmer's wife. After living in the foster care system, Emma finally had a home. The thing she'd longed for since middle school.

A wave of panic at losing this delightful plot of land and everything that came with it squeezed her chest and made it difficult to breathe. If she was forced to sell their little homestead on the outskirts of Serenity, Texas, where would they live? And if they didn't have Jubilee Farm, then she'd no longer have the family store and the income she was developing to allow her to build the financial security she craved. She blinked away the sudden tears that filled her eyes.

"You okay?" Carter asked as Addie wiggled from her arms and toddled off to play with her siblings. The limp appeared gone. Her doctor had said her symptoms would come and go. So far, her little one had been doing so well with this expensive medication.

"Not really."

She fingered the heart necklace Robbie had gifted her right before his diagnosis.

Their dream of raising their children here might very well come crashing down if she couldn't find an affordable medical plan to carry them. There had to be another option other than selling the farm or going into more credit card debt every month to pay for the medicine. But what?

Two days later, Carter pushed open Emma's teal blue front door as thunder cracked behind him. Earlier he had sent her a text about coming over and she'd replied to let himself in. He was greeted with Mikey's wail resounding from the back of the house. But it wasn't an *I'm hurt* cry, more like an *I want attention and no one is giving it to me* fussy sob.

Carter strode into the kitchen and put Emma's favorite iced-coffee drink on the messy counter. Was this offering to sweeten her up for the discussion they were about to have? Maybe. He swallowed the nervous lump in his throat and wiped his sweaty palms on his blue jeans.

Emma's revelation about her medical insurance situation and inability to pay for Addie's medicine had left Carter with an overwhelming sense of dread. The notion that Emma might go bankrupt to keep her child healthy panicked him. He couldn't believe this specialized drug was so costly, but even with a nice salary, he couldn't afford to loan Emma the money she would need every month for the prescription.

Ever since their last discussion, he'd been preoccupied with this dilemma and had shuttered himself in his bungalow, working and praying. Last night, he'd come up with a plan and had spent the night in prayer, asking for wisdom and guidance. This morning his chest swelled with a sense of absolute certainty this plan had come from God, not Carter.

Now he just had to get Emma to agree to marry someone with a medical plan like he had. Then the man could include her and the triplets as dependents on his insurance at work. It was the perfect idea.

As Mikey's crying roared, he poured her drink into a spill-proof tumbler, made his way to the sunroom in the back of the home and slipped through the baby gate. His chest ached for the boy, but he was unsure if he should comfort him or ignore him, like his mother was doing right now.

Emma sat on one of the two long couches in shorts, a T-shirt and bare feet, her summer uniform. Though tending after triplets and a goat farm, she still always looked radiant and amazing. Her cheeks were flushed, like she'd been working hard today, and her hair was in a loose ponytail. She blew a strand of long blond hair from her face and shot a smile his way. Cassie, the oldest of the feisty three-year-old triplets, snuggled beside her with a board book sitting between them. Addie, the littlest, climbed on the arm of the couch and peered under her mother's elbow at the horses on the page. Emma said something, and the girls giggled. The sweet sound almost brought him to his knees, though he could barely hear their joyous laughter over Mikey's howls.

Mikey lay next to the sturdy train table. His face was bright red, his cheeks smeared with dirty tears and he kept glancing at his mother to see if he'd gotten her attention yet. As Emma remained engrossed in the book and the girls, he stuck out his lower lip and threw another small train toward the empty couch where a pile of discarded toys lay, nearly hitting the rain-splattered windows.

Then Mikey rolled over and spied Carter. His lips turned upside down as he quieted and sent the sweetest smile in Carter's direction. Carter's heart melted at the expression. He knew he shouldn't have favorites, but something about this little boy had stolen his affections when he'd first met the tot as a baby.

Mikey sat up and patted the hardwood floor beside him. "Here," he said, indicating for Carter to sit next to him. The boy swiped the wetness off his face, creating dirty swirls on his chubby cheeks. They must have been outside this morning before the rains began.

Carter gulped at the invitation. His arthritis was acting up today and there was no way he could lower himself to the floor and sit, though he'd love to. He'd been diagnosed with early onset osteoarthritis at eighteen, as a freshman in college. Now, over ten years later, his symptoms had progressed, but he'd learned what movements caused pain and avoided them.

He grinned at Mikey then placed Emma's drink on the small table beside her. A citrus and vanilla scent emanated from her like she'd just showered. He strode over to Mikey, lifted the fearless boy in the air and flew him in a circle, staying clear of the toy trains underfoot. His hands cramped up, but as long as he kept a solid hold on the child and Mikey was happy, a little discomfort was worth it.

Mikey laughed with glee and his face

was no longer red. Hopefully, his little tantrum was behind him.

As Carter set the boy on his feet, he said, "Again, Unkie C, again."

The girls spotted Carter and came running, their little feet pounding against the hardwood floor beneath them. He promised Mikey he'd fly him one more time after he greeted the girls. Knowing he couldn't crouch low, he settled on a nearby glider and the girls scurried over to him. They both clamored for his neck. Cassie landed on his right, chattering away. Addie settled on his left, content to have her sister monopolize the conversation. He was thrilled the doctors had been able to diagnose her and get her the medicine she needed so quickly, though the weeklong hospital stay and month of tests and follow-up appointments hadn't felt quick at the time.

Emma lifted her drink in a toast and mouthed, *Thank you*. Her lips were ruby-red. She always looked like she had lipstick on, but he was pretty sure it was all natural. She took a sip and her tense shoulders sagged as she relished the unexpected treat. For the moment, she might be happy, but his proposition would likely shock her.

After he extracted himself from the girls, he went over to Emma, who'd started collecting toys in a laundry basket. "We need to talk. Privately," he said.

She looked at him with a startled expression in her ocean-blue eyes and then scrutinized the heavy rains outside. She nodded, set the triplets up with a short video and settled on the couch with her feet curled under her and her coveted coffee drink clutched in her grasp.

He strode over to the couch and shook out his sore hands while praying for the right words and that Emma would at least consider his idea.

"I've been praying ever since we talked the other day about the insurance situation," he started. Her eyes filled with anguish and her lips quivered at the mention of the subject. "You should marry someone to get the insurance you need." He ignored the shock that covered her face and bulldozed forward. "It only makes sense. Addie needs medical insurance and, as you said, my plan, like lots of tech companies', is gold-plated. There's nothing they don't cover."

She jumped up. "You're crazy," she shot back in a low voice. "You want me to marry a complete stranger for medical insurance?" She glanced at the children, who were still engrossed with the short video.

"Well, it could be someone you know. There are several single guys who live in Serenity and work remotely for Conrad Vaughn. His company has great benefits."

"This is insane, Carter." She paced the length of the couch and back, keeping her voice low. "When I married Robbie, that was it. My one true love." She worried her lower lip between her teeth.

Of course, she was still in love with her

late husband and always would be. Understandable. "This would be a marriage of convenience only. Love wouldn't enter the equation."

She stopped her pacing and gave him a quick shake of the head. "No, Carter, that won't work. You know I don't trust many people. And now you think we should hunt for some single guy with great medical insurance who'll marry me?"

He hadn't given any thought to Emma's trust issues. He'd been more focused on coming up with a short list of candidates. The one thing he knew was that his name couldn't be on the list.

She set her drink on the side table and sank onto the couch, head in her hands. "If you didn't recommend marrying a complete stranger, it's not a bad idea," she mumbled.

Carter bit his tongue while he gave Emma time to mull over the proposal.

She faced him, perched on the edge of her seat. "Why do you think we should search for a complete stranger? Why not you?" Her head jerked back. "I'm sorry, Carter, forgive me, that was much too forward."

But as a friend, she deserved to know why he wasn't in the running. He felt obliged to share the secret only his parents and doctor knew.

"At eighteen, I was having joint issues with my knees. My doctor diagnosed me with early onset osteoarthritis."

Her eyes widened. "Carter, I'm so sorry."

He was embarrassed about his diagnosis, which was the reason he hadn't told anyone. He didn't want people to treat him differently. "Well, now you understand. I don't want to burden you, or anyone, with my condition."

"Is that why you always say you're a bachelor 'til the rapture?"

He nodded. A partial reason he planned to remain a bachelor was that he didn't want to saddle a wife with his disease. But the painful breakup in college also counted. It had been eight years since Madison had dumped him because of his medical condition, but she'd made her lasting mark.

"You should have told me when we got Addie's diagnosis, it would have helped me see someone fully functioning and all."

He barked out a wry laugh. He wouldn't describe himself as "fully functioning." Each year, his flexibility decreased, and he lived in pain daily. "It's a different arthritis."

"I've been thinking diet and supplements might help Addie further. Maybe we can work together to help her, and you, feel better."

He didn't want to tell her what the doctor had informed him to expect. So far, he'd been right. Carter hoped Addie would grow out of her ailment. "I'll do whatever I can for Addie. For any of the children. You know that."

He leaned against the soft couch cushion, considering his two childhood dreams.

One was to be a rancher, like his dad, but when the stiffness had started as a teenager, he'd known that riding horses for hours at a time wasn't in his future, which shattered that dream. The second was to be a husband and father, but his disease would be too much of a hardship for a wife.

"On the surface," she said, "a marriage of convenience is not a bad idea and, other than selling this beloved farm, it might be the only option on the table." Yet uncertainty remained on her face. "For starters, it isn't biblical."

"I actually think a marriage of convenience can be," he retorted. He'd been thinking about this all night. His faith was important to him, just like Emma. "If we find the right guy, say someone not interested in marrying for his own reasons, then they'll be committed to remain married for life."

She hugged herself as though she were cold. Either the iced drink had chilled her or she was seriously considering his idea and was panicked. Based on the faraway look and the rapid blinking, he'd guess the idea of remarrying was freaking her out. Sure, not a decision to be taken lightly, but he knew a few guys at church with great benefits who had stated they were never getting married. If she agreed, he'd open with asking those two.

She turned to him, her knee rapidly bouncing, and swallowed as though nervous. "The show is almost over." She nodded to the television. "Listen." She unwrapped her arms and clasped her hands in front of her while quieting her knee as though she had something important to say. Good, she'd finally accepted his idea had merit. "You never plan to marry. I had my one true love with Robbie. It's an option to consider."

His eyes widened as he pressed his palms toward her to stop her crazy talk. No, this wasn't the plan at all. She deserved much better than him, someone whole. "I told you about my disease. I'd be a burden to you, Emma. You don't want me."

"I don't want anyone except Robbie," she snapped, "but here we are." The lines on her forehead creased in worry. "If I marry for insurance, it isn't going to be some random guy, Carter, it'll be you. I know you. I trust you."

His chest tightened and he couldn't seem to get enough breath into his lungs. If he'd learned only one thing from Madison, it was that no one wanted him.

Emma didn't understand. This was forever, and she deserved better than him.

Chapter Two

The next afternoon, Emma pocketed her phone, giddy the baker from Love Valley was on board to sell her mouthwatering pecan pies and red velvet cakes on commission. A light in this daze of trying to figure out what to do about Addie's medication. After all the farm expenses, the family store was barely breaking even. Adding the desserts would tip the balance sheet to profitable and she wouldn't have to dip into her meager savings every month to make ends meet. For someone who had dyscalculia, a math disability, that was a huge win. She grinned as excitement and hope threaded through her core.

Emma found a shady spot and locked the triplet stroller with her three-year-olds buckled in. Mikey munched on pretzel goldfish, Cassie watched a children's show on her handheld toddler tablet and Addie was sound asleep in the last seat. She swept Addie's bangs away from her closed eyes and felt her forehead for a moment, thankful their littlest was healthy after a rough couple of months. It was rare that Emma could wrangle the three of them in the stroller so she could do chores, so she'd better get started.

She scooped goat pellets into the feeding pail and let herself into the boys' pen, securing the gate closed behind her. The medical insurance dilemma came to mind. Now that the baker from Love Valley was on board, it seemed like a sign that Emma shouldn't sell her property, not with the family store about to become profitable. But, unfortunately, the baked goods profits wouldn't put a dent in the cost of Addie's monthly medication.

She poured pellets in both feed buckets. Chewie raced to his food while Emma crouched low to hug Mr. Prancer, her husband's pride and joy. Their first goat purchase had been a great one since he'd come from good milk lines and had gorgeous blue eyes, the current craze that customers loved. Robbie had picked out the buck and named him. Prancer rested his chin on her shoulder and nibbled at her hair like he'd done so many times before. She relished the sweet moment because this was where she felt closest to Robbie, but her heavy thoughts soon returned.

Should she marry Carter?

She'd exhausted all the other options. Although she hadn't intended to remarry, Carter's idea made sense, and it might be her only option, assuming he was willing.

Except, marriage was a lifetime commitment made to one another and God, and she wasn't sure God would agree with their scheme. What if Carter changed his mind at some point and wanted out? Where would that leave her and the triplets?

The crunch of tires over gravel sounded and Carter's sedan pulled in. Just the man she needed to speak with. She waved at him as he stepped out of his car then she rushed through feeding the girl goats.

She'd have to come back later to finish. She slipped out of the pen and released the children from their confines. Cassie and Mikey raced to Carter while Emma snuggled with Addie, who was still sleepy from her nap.

Carter tipped Mikey upside down. The spectacle sent Cassie into a frenzy of giggles until he grabbed her up in his arms, laughing. The sight softened Emma's heart. She could hardly imagine the love and support he would offer as a husband.

They moved to the backyard. Carter put Mikey and Cassie on the swings and gently pushed them. Since the triplets were new to these swings, they were still learning how to hold the ropes and stay on, so the rule was to stay low.

After Emma placed Addie in the third swing, she joined him. He was much taller than her five-foot-four frame. She concentrated on the children, his marriage of convenience weighing on her mind.

"What are you thinking about?"

She glanced at him, the thick hair around his face lifted with the breeze. "You know."

When Mikey hopped off the swing, she and Carter picked up the girls and set them gently on the ground, knowing they'd want to follow their brother. All three rushed off to the patio cushion container where Mikey had seen a salamander earlier in the day. They each got a stick to search for the reptile.

"You shouldn't give up on love just because I need medical insurance," she stated.

His features hardened as he swallowed.

Clearly, this wasn't a topic he was comfortable discussing. "I fell in love in college and the breakup really hurt." He kept his focus on the children so she couldn't see his eyes, but she could hear the agony radiating from his words. "I decided a few years ago that I didn't want to go through that pain again. That, coupled with my disease, is the full reason I have remained a bachelor."

By the hurt in his voice, she could tell there was much more to his story than that brief explanation. But at least that slice of information allayed her fears. He'd decided not to marry well before her need for medical insurance had become an issue. And, just like her, he had no plans to fall in love again.

But what about her? When she had ended up in foster care, everything had changed. She'd learned not to rely on anyone but herself. Life was more predictable that way. When Robbie came along, he was safe because he was a fellow orphan.

But Carter? If they married, she'd have to make sure she remained self-reliant.

"God put the marriage of convenience notion on my heart. That's why I proposed the idea yesterday." His voice was so soft she almost had to lean in. "Even though I am not the best option for a husband, by any stretch, I can see how marrying would benefit both of us. You'd get the medical insurance you need and I'd get to be a father. Something I thought I'd never have."

She was unsure about remarrying, but she had exhausted all other options. And since she had trust issues, Carter was the only person she'd consider. She was grateful he was offering himself up, especially because he was already a good friend, yet this felt wrong on so many levels.

The sudden cacophony of bleating turned her attention to the spacious goat yard and the promise it held.

"Carter, if we decide to…marry, you need to know how important Jubilee Farm is to me."

"I understand. You have registered and papered goats. I know how much you get for every kid and it's impressive." She blushed at his acknowledgment. Maybe a marriage to Carter would work.

"Thank you. I know to some it may seem like a hobby but, along with our survivor benefits, it's the funds that keep us going. If we marry, I don't want your money. None of it."

He nodded, a solemn look covering his face.

"Maybe more importantly, other than Addie, Cassie and Mikey, this goat farm connects me to Robbie."

"I know it's more than the goats and chickens and family store. You and Robbie had an extensive plan for this place. No matter what happens, I support you in this venture."

Now for the big question. "What would Robbie think about us marrying?" she whispered.

Carter turned to her, his features full of

compassion, as though he understood how hard this decision would be for her, considering her love for Robbie. "I think he'd rather you marry someone than go bankrupt to keep Addie healthy." He furrowed his brow. "How about we meet with Pastor Tony?"

"Maybe." This was an enormous decision. Speaking with their pastor would certainly help.

But she couldn't get over how marrying Carter might taint what she'd had with Robbie.

Cassie let out a giggle and Emma looked over at the triplets' quest to find the salamander. If she married Carter, would her children forget their father?

There had to be a better choice than either marrying Carter or selling Jubilee Farm because neither seemed ideal.

The next afternoon, Carter stood on Emma's front stoop, dotted with healthy ferns in rustic containers, and took a deep breath. Today might change his life forever. He tried to ignore the quiver in his chest that was from either nervousness or excitement. When Emma had first insisted they marry, he'd been stunned. Even panicked. But after some heavy-duty praying, God had given him peace because the thought of marrying Emma no longer scared the daylights out of him.

He pushed open the teal blue door as Emma pulled the knob on the other side. He fell forward, catching himself before he face-planted.

She stepped back. "I said I'd meet you in the car," Emma muttered.

He righted himself and tried to hold the door for her, but she was on the porch quicker than a jackrabbit running from a predator.

He could hear the triplets from the back of the house whining about Emma leaving. They still struggled on Sunday mornings in the church nursery, but today they were in excellent hands with Carter's mother, who was their pseudo grandmother. He shut the door and pressed the keypad to lock it.

Emma stood next to his sedan, tapping her sandal-clad toes, as though she were impatient to get going. He hurried over. Today she wore nice jeans, a crisp T-shirt, a cross-body purse and pink sandals that highlighted an intricate flower between her toes.

Except, Carter detected uncertainty in her wide eyes. But when their gazes met, she nodded. Her chin firming in that decisive way she had about her. She slid into the passenger seat of his sedan before he had a chance to open her door.

He settled in the driver's seat, disappointed she wouldn't allow him to be the gentleman he was raised to be. When he glanced at her, he almost asked if she was sure she wanted to do this, but he kept his mouth closed. Marriage was something neither of them wanted. But something she needed. And he'd get to be a husband and father out of the bargain.

"Let's do this," she said then graced him with a smile, but the corners of her lips didn't quite reach her eyes. He got it. This decision was life-altering.

He started the car and headed toward downtown Serenity, specifically First Church and the scheduled meeting with their pastor. Frankly, marrying Emma was perfect for him because he didn't plan on falling in love again. It hurt too much. With Emma, there would be no emotions to keep in check.

"I think Prancer is finally getting used to Chewie," she said.

A few months back, she'd lost a buck to the coyote, and a friend had given her a neutered male to keep Prancer company. For a while, it had done the opposite because Prancer either ignored Chewie or slammed his head against the neutered male's side when he wasn't paying attention.

"How so?" Carter asked.

"This morning I fed the girl goats first, and they were standing side by side waiting for me. Prancer didn't try anything funny, even when he finished eating first. Definitely a step in the right direction."

"Glad to hear that." He slowed as he neared downtown.

"Oh, in all this focus on medical insurance, I forgot to tell you that the baker from Love Valley has agreed to sell her pecan pies and red velvet cakes at the family store." She grinned as she tucked a loose lock of hair behind her ear. She'd worn her long blond hair down in waves today and looked especially gorgeous.

"Congratulations, Emma, that's great news." Though she didn't make a ton of money, it wasn't anything to sneeze at.

She had started the family store as a way to offset the farm expenditures. Any expenses for the chickens and goats were paid by the family store profits. They had been in business for six years and had just recently become profitable, by a narrow margin.

Robbie would be so proud of her. She

had been through a lot with her husband's illness and death, followed quickly by Addie's sickness and medical diagnosis. Now she was taking the bull by the horns with deciding about a marriage of convenience. If she agreed to go through with it and chose Carter, he'd be honored to help her out. He pulled into the church lot and parked.

After settling in Pastor Tony's guest chairs, Carter explained the dilemma with Addie's medical insurance and his harebrained marriage bargain idea. Their pastor stared at them for a moment and then prayed for their upcoming conversation.

"Based on what Carter has proposed, I'm considering this discussion a premarital counseling session," Pastor Tony said. "We can meet as many times as necessary before the two of you are comfortable with whatever final decision you make. Emma, what are your thoughts?"

"Since Robbie was my one true love, and I know I'll never fall in love again, I think Carter's marriage of convenience is smart, but I want to get your biblical take on the arrangement."

Pastor Tony nodded. "Would the two of you plan on divorcing at any point, say, when the children go to college? Or are you going into this arrangement committed to the marriage for your lifetime?"

"I'll never get divorced." She glanced at Carter. "I'm going into this fully committed. Of course, we wouldn't have a real marriage in every sense of the word." Heat climbed up her neck and settled on her cheeks. "But other than that, I'd honor all the other marriage commitments in front of God. For life."

She was adorable, all embarrassed over there.

"That's good to hear, Emma. Your intentions sound God-honoring." The pastor's eyes crinkled at the corners. "Now, Carter, what are your plans for the future? Do you see divorce as an option?"

His mind went straight to Madison, his

college sweetheart, and the day he'd told her about his arthritis and how the disease might affect his body over his lifetime. He had loved her deeply and couldn't imagine a future without her, so he'd wanted to inform her of his ailment before he'd proposed. When she'd looked at him with an icy stare and told him she was looking for a healthy husband, she'd crushed him. Then she'd declared it'd be best if they parted ways. Told him it might be hard for a little while, but in the long term he'd thank her.

That day, he had decided love wasn't for him. His broken heart had taken years to mend. Some days he wondered if he was over the heartbreak yet. A few years ago, he'd gone on a couple of dates with a woman he'd liked, only to find out she was dating another man. They hadn't had an exclusive relationship, but the experience reminded him that love hurt. So, he had resolved that the wisest and safest choice would be to remain single.

"I hadn't planned on marriage. I'm one of those 'bachelor 'til the rapture' guys." He gave the pastor a crooked smile and hoped the man wouldn't dig deeper. "Since I hadn't planned on love, I am comfortable marrying and committing for life."

Helping raise the children would be the straightforward part of this arrangement. Emma would be the tough nut to crack because somehow he'd have to break through her *I don't need help* façade and be a useful helpmate for her, the triplets, the farm and the family store.

Pastor Tony asked them a few more questions but seemed satisfied with their intentions to honor God, even though their marriage would be one of convenience.

He offered to marry them in a private ceremony, but Emma stated she hadn't made a final decision. And if they followed through, she preferred a justice of the peace.

They left his office through a side door and quietly settled in Carter's sedan.

Even though he knew Emma could do better than him, his mother was confident that if Carter and Emma married and remained committed to their marriage, they would fall in love and live happily ever after.

Carter shook his head at his mother's romantic notion. She read far too many romance novels.

Neither he nor Emma was looking for love. Assuming Emma would even accept this crazy whirlwind proposal.

A buzzing noise woke Emma. Groggy, she rolled over in the dark and checked the two monitors. The baby monitor showed no movement. Next, she looked at the tablet displaying the goat pens. The motion detector had turned the floodlight on. Her eyes widened and she sat up.

She flung the blankets off, threw on a light sweater and grabbed her phone. She raced outside and spotted a figure in the distance running away. About the size of a coyote. Her heart rate spiked.

Since Carter also got the alerts on his phone, she shot him a text message to let him know she was taking care of the coyote issue and not to worry. Then she rushed over to the goat pens.

Prancer stood in the corner, facing where the coyote had run from. Since he wasn't snorting and stomping, he probably hadn't seen the coyote, just heard him. When Emma reached the buck, she whispered to him. He turned and flung his head at her, acknowledging her presence, and seemed to go from alert to watchful. Even though there was a nice raised bed in their pen, Chewie was sound asleep on an old wooden pallet that was missing half the boards. She smiled and gave Prancer a pat before turning her attention to the females.

She let herself into their pen and closed the gate with a trembling hand before moving through and counting the does.

Grace, the self-appointed herd leader, was keeping her eye out for trouble but probably hadn't even heard the coyote come near. Maybe the motion-detecting light had done the trick and spooked the coyote off. Emma added up all the girls. Her legs were wobbly until she reached her magic number: twenty-one. She heaved a sigh of relief that none of her goats had been snatched. *Thank You, Lord, for protecting my herd once again. And for waking me.*

Just yesterday, a customer had picked up the final spring kid. The last time she'd had a coyote roam around at night, the mamas were in a separate pen and had herded the babies into a corner to guard them. Tonight, most of the females were bedded down. Only three seemed to be in paroling mode right now.

Tires crunched over gravel, breaking the silence, and she turned toward the noise. Had Carter actually come here? She hadn't meant for him to. The reason she'd sent him a text was so he would know she had the situation under control. She moved to the driveway as his sedan rolled up. She tugged her sweater closed, embarrassed she had pajamas on. Well, workout shorts and one of Robbie's old T-shirts, but still.

He exited the car and softly closed the door. "Everything okay?" he whispered.

Man, he'd gotten here in just a few minutes from his bungalow in downtown Serenity. He must have jumped out of bed and raced to his car as soon as he'd received her message. She rested her palm on his upper arm, thankful for everything about the man.

"Yes. I've accounted for all the herd. I think Prancer may have heard the coyote, but I don't think he saw him." She used both hands to wrap her sweater a little tighter.

"Maybe that means it didn't get too close."

"I'm hoping the motion-detector light frightened him off." Except, what if the screen door slapping against the frame had done the trick? "What if he's hiding in the shadows, waiting for me to go inside so he can return?"

"I don't think wild animals have such deep thoughts." His eyes twinkled. "Anyway, my sister should get the dogs here soon. Then the training can start."

The thought of trained dogs to guard the herd calmed her for the moment. "Of course, it'll take a few more months before they're fully trained." Boy, was she thankful there was a dog trainer in the family. Autumn Nelson and her husband, Wyatt, had secured two dogs that were currently going through a generalized training program. Emma couldn't wait until the dogs were here, then she'd be one step closer to not having a coyote problem.

"You should go home. I'm sorry you rushed over for a false alarm."

"It wasn't a false alarm. There was a coyote. I'm glad everything turned out okay." He started toward his car, then looked over his shoulder. "You'll be able to fall back asleep, right?"

"Of course." Though, to be honest, she wouldn't be able to sleep knowing the coyote was out there close by.

He faced her. "You'll lie awake, worried. I just know it."

She glanced at her phone. "I've already had four hours of sleep, so—"

"You have triplets. You need your sleep." He clicked the button on his remote to lock his car and then climbed up onto the front porch. "I'll turn the alert notification on high and wait for daybreak right here." He settled on a rocker that she knew wasn't too comfortable.

She looked over her shoulder at the herd. He was right. She'd never fall back asleep. But with Carter on her porch guarding, she'd sleep like a baby. She tugged her sweater tighter as indecision warred within. She didn't need to be watched over like a child. But having him there tonight sure would be nice.

"Are you sure?" she asked. "Maybe I can get you a blanket or a bottle of water?"

"Nope, I'm good." He tapped his phone, then turned it to her. "Notifications are on high. Get some shut-eye, okay?"

She felt bad he wouldn't get a good night's sleep, but he was right—triplets were exhausting. Knowing he was there would allow her to be refreshed in the morning, but she had to make sure she didn't abuse their friendship.

She let herself in the kitchen door and kicked off her muck boots while considering the meeting with Pastor Tony earlier in the day. After hearing his words of wisdom, their next step wasn't so scary. And, frankly, between selling Jubilee Farm or marrying Carter for insurance, Robbie would want her choosing the marriage of convenience.

Anyway, Carter's college heartbreak made her more comfortable to move forward. With Robbie in her heart, she'd never fall in love again. And since Carter had been burned enough for a lifetime, there were no risks entering into marriage with him.

Robbie had always trusted Carter. Now it was her turn.

Satisfied by her final decision and with Carter keeping watch over the herd, she should sleep like a baby.

The following morning, she stepped onto the porch where Carter was asleep. When she spoke, he startled. "Sorry, didn't mean to wake you," Emma said as she gazed at Carter's contorted face, probably sore from the unforgiving rocker. "I'm sorry you had to sleep on the porch. It must have been so uncomfortable." Her stomach twisted at the thought of the conversation ahead of them. Was he still willing to marry her?

"Are the children awake?" he asked in a gravelly voice then cleared his throat.

"Not yet, but I have the baby monitor app on high." She gazed across her farmyard, chewing on her bottom lip. How do you accept a marriage of convenience proposal? And was it still on the table?

"Everything okay?" he asked. Why was he sitting there so stiffly? Didn't he want to stand and stretch after spending the night on that hard rocker?

She turned her attention back to the goats. "I'm worried about that coyote. Last time he came around, he was persistent until we added the additional fencing. I'm just afraid he's going to keep coming back. What if he's successful?"

"He won't be." Carter started to straighten and then winced. Oh my, he was sore. Last night when he had offered to stay, she should have remembered about his arthritis.

"How about I move into the RV," Carter said, "like I did while you and Addie were in the hospital? I'll keep the motion alert notification on high and chase him away when he shows up."

Her eyes widened. "No, Carter. Goodness, what was I thinking? I don't want to impose on you."

"You aren't imposing. I'm offering. Anyway, you have to care for triplets every day. The least I can do is handle the herd at night." He shifted but pain covered his face and he froze. Was it just normal discomfort from sleeping on the unforgiving chair or was his arthritis bothering him? "At least until the dogs are trained and ready to protect the herd. Autumn says it'll only be a couple of months."

Tension bunching up in her shoulders released with his offer. She hadn't realized how concerned she was about the coyote until Carter had given her a solution.

"The RV isn't very comfortable for a lengthy period," she said. "You should take the guest room. It's on the other side of the house and has its own bathroom and everything." Though it would be weird to have him in the house...but that'd be better than him trying to sleep on that uncomfortable RV mattress.

His eyebrows lifted in surprise at her suggestion. "The RV works for me. I'll just get a top of the line foam mattress. If I order this morning, it'll be here tomorrow." He gave her a nod, as though the arrangements had been settled.

"If you're sure." She dug her fingertips against her forehead and massaged what felt like the beginnings of a migraine. Now, for the tough part. She prayed for the right words and focused on the sun as it moved higher in the sky. The chickens clucked and the goats bleated, giving her comfort as she soaked in the peacefulness of Jubilee Farm.

She took a deep breath and then spoke. "I've made a decision." She turned to him, determined now. "If you're still willing, I'd like to marry you." She flinched at her brazen words, hoping he wouldn't take them out of context. "Because of the medical insurance and all that."

He gave her a small smile, his eyes crinkling at the corners. He appeared pleased.

"I'll contact the justice of the peace in Love Valley, like we talked about, and let you know the details."

She felt like she should hug him or something, but he remained stiff as a board in the chair. Was he hurting? She shook her head. She had too much on her plate to worry about Carter's aches and pains. He was an adult. She had three little ones to tend to.

She pressed her hand over her heart. "Thank you, Carter, for everything." Addie's medication would be covered from now on. Emma wanted to pump her fist in delight. One less expense to fret over.

After thanking him again, she slipped into the house and leaned against the wooden front door. The silence enveloped her.

Had she made the right decision? She pressed her eyes closed and felt peace. *Thank You, Lord.*

Later on, after the children had woken, she prepared a simple breakfast while the triplets chattered away. Right then, the severity of her marriage decision caught her off guard.

Would Carter expect to be included in more parts of her life other than spending time with the triplets? Hopefully, he understood they were making a trade—she and the triplets would receive the medical insurance they so desperately needed and he would be a father.

As long as he didn't nose into other parts of her life. Because she had everything under control and didn't need help from anyone.

Chapter Three

Carter rolled over and squinted at the morning light glinting through the shutters covering his bedroom windows. His stomach clenched. Today was his wedding day, the day he and Emma would stand in front of a magistrate and become legally bound to each other. Forever. Indecision warred. Emma could do so much better than him. His chest gave a tight squeeze at the predicament he was in. He smacked the off button on his old-school alarm clock before the buzzing started and gave him a headache.

When she'd first announced her decision, he'd been thrilled. Addie needed a prescription plan and, frankly, Emma's entire family could use solid medical insurance rather than the flimsy plan she had in place. But him?

He shook his head and then groaned at the ache in his neck from lying in a bad position overnight, which was odd because he had tossed and turned all night. Although, he must have fallen asleep at some point to get this annoying crick in his neck.

He swung his legs over the side of the bed and rolled out his stiff shoulders. A sleepless night always made him feel like an eighty-year-old man, not a twenty-nine-year-old. All he wanted to do was crawl back in bed and get some restful sleep, but their nine o'clock appointment with the Hope Valley justice of the peace loomed.

Instead of a hopeful attitude toward his upcoming nuptials, Carter's throat tightened at the torment growing in his belly. Emma should be marrying someone who wasn't broken. How had he let this situation come so far? Since she'd agreed to marry him, he'd been so busy that he hadn't given himself time to think. He allowed the huge life decision a moment to settle. He was going to be a husband and father. Soon.

His pulse stuttered at the exciting development. Two roles he never thought he would be able to fulfill. But, just as quick, he questioned if it was too late to call the whole thing off and find someone healthier for her to marry. No, he couldn't do that to Addie or Emma. They were counting on him. Maybe he wasn't the best pick for Emma, but she had chosen him.

Though Robbie had asked him to watch over Emma and the triplets, his best friend hadn't known about his arthritis. Carter knew he couldn't keep up with the triplets and probably wouldn't be much help on the farm. Anyway, Madison had told him he wasn't a great communicator, so marriage? He shook his head at the situation he'd found himself in.

He moved toward the kitchen to make some breakfast and passed his home office with his ergonomic desk and chair. He paused in the doorway. Those items that kept him comfortable during work hours would not fit in the RV. Maybe he could bring his office chair, but not the rest.

He massaged his aching palms. Was he selfish to not want to give all this up when he'd worked so hard to get himself into an environment where he was able to coddle his symptoms? He hoped his arthritis would not get worse living in the RV.

He fixed a quick breakfast then made a mental note to ask his brothers to help move his office chair soon. As he settled in his sedan, a sense of foreboding came over him. *Lord, am I doing the right thing by marrying Emma? Did I step in front of Your Will because I was excited at the idea of being a husband and father?*

An awareness that he needed to pray overtook him, so he chose the long route to Emma's. As he drove, he prayed to the

One he trusted. At some point, he remembered Pastor Tony had told them that marriage was hard work. And that it was a choice. With each mile that ticked on his odometer, the heaviness he'd felt about the day disappeared. *Thank You, Lord.*

When he arrived at Emma's, his mother's car was tucked at the end of the drive, so he knew the triplets were being watched. An unfamiliar car was parked in front of the family store. Should he pull around the customer and just wait for Emma or go in and try to help? As he rubbed a hand over his freshly shaven face, Esther Woodward stepped out of the family store, looking around. Before the older woman spotted him, Emma strode past his sedan, tapped the window and waved hi. She then greeted Esther with a hug.

Well, now that Emma knew he'd arrived, he couldn't sit there like a slug. He unfolded himself from the vehicle and entered the little store. Maybe he could be of some help.

"Good morning, Mrs. Woodward," he said, feeling awkward as all get out that he and Emma were about to marry and no one other than his family knew. What would everyone say about their quick marriage? Though, maybe Esther already knew since she came over for a few hours every Wednesday to watch the triplets for Emma. They seemed pretty close.

"Look at you, all gussied up," Esther stated, then turned her attention to Emma. "And you are lovely. Is that new?" The older woman was right. Emma looked stunning in a floral sundress.

Emma's chin dipped down and she pressed her lips together, as though embarrassed by the new clothing. "Yes. Autumn and I went on a little shopping trip the other day." She had gone shopping with his sister? How had he missed that? "What can I help you with, Esther?"

"Earl wants some rib eye steaks. I'll take four today." A local cattle rancher sold his beef in Emma's store and she got a nice commission off each purchase.

Emma nodded, moving over to the deep freezer that held the beef. "Do you want to pick them out?" He couldn't help but notice the rings missing from her left ring finger. The empty, grooved space was lily-white compared to the rest of her tanned skin.

"No, dear, you can," Esther said as she rubbed her elbow. "And I've hurt my arm, so can you put them on my front seat? Earl said he'd pack them in the freezer when I get home." Her husband was the town veterinarian, and their home was close to his clinic.

Emma picked up the meat and went to Esther's car, the door slapping behind her.

"And some eggs." Esther eyed the farm-fresh egg carton options. Since Emma wasn't there at the moment, Carter moved to the desk to help. "I'll take one of the mixed six-packs." She pointed as Emma returned. Well, he was about to become her husband and helpmate, so he might as well learn how to help in her store.

He picked up the egg pack from the display and turned to hand it to Esther. Though he thought he had a good grip on it, his hand cramped and before he could save it, the container slipped to the table with a thud. The now-cracked eggs started to run out of the cardboard carton onto the rustic-wood tabletop that Emma used as her checkout area. The colorful shells swam in the clear liquid, mocking him. All because of his stupid arthritis. How could he bungle something as simple as selling eggs to someone? And if he couldn't handle such a basic task, then how was he supposed to be an adequate helpmate?

"Oh dear," Esther stated.

"Let me get that," Emma said as she came to his rescue and cleaned up the egg disaster. She shot him a sweet smile and gave Esther fresh eggs, but Carter knew she had to be disappointed in his blunder. He sure was. She checked Esther out and sent her on her way with a tight goodbye hug. But when Emma turned from the door, her features were strained. Either she was nervous about the upcoming wedding or questioning if she should marry him.

The peace he'd felt as he'd driven into her driveway fled away. He didn't blame her if she changed her mind. She should marry someone who could be a helpmate rather than someone who'd be a hindrance to her.

Sure, studies showed his lifespan wouldn't theoretically be cut short because of arthritis, but what if he became a burden to Emma? That was the last thing he wanted.

"'Til death do us part," the justice of the peace said, his baritone voice echoing in the empty courtroom.

Emma Bailey gulped as her pulse skittered at the sacred words. Was she doing the right thing? After Robbie passed, she never thought she'd marry again, but with Addie needing that expensive medicine, she didn't have a choice. *God, why did You take Robbie from us?*

It had only been three days since the latest coyote scare and the night she'd decided to enter this marriage of convenience. Except, this all felt like it was happening too fast. But since Addie's medication refill date was coming up soon, action had to be taken.

She leaned into Carter, so only he'd hear her. "Are you sure?"

He gave her one assured nod. His chin was set and firm, seemingly certain about their modern-day marriage of convenience decision. Taking confidence from him and the discussion they'd had with their pastor, she repeated the words.

"Do you have the rings?" The magistrate asked Carter, who'd gotten a haircut sometime in the past few days. The little curl at the base of his neck was gone, replaced by a crisp cut. He was tall, dark and handsome, and one of the sweetest men she knew besides Robbie. And he had a large, loving family that she adored. She didn't deserve him. She knew it.

She wiped her sweaty palms against the soft floral fabric of her sundress.

Carter patted both dress pants' pockets before pulling out the simple bands they'd purchased earlier on their way into Love Valley. They lived in Serenity, Texas, but their hometown was too small for a justice of the peace, which was probably a good thing because she was uncomfortable with everyone knowing their marital status. At least right away. She needed their new situation to sink in before sharing with others.

She held out her shaking hand to Carter as her almost-husband repeated the magistrate's words.

"With this ring, I take you as my wife, for as long as we both shall live," Carter said, his chocolate eyes resolute in that promise.

A week ago, those words had concerned her, but when they'd met with Pastor Tony, he'd eased her worries. He'd assured them that as long as they lived up to the promise to stay together, they would not be making a mockery of marriage. He had also reminded them that marriage wasn't easy. They'd have to work hard at their relationship and communication skills, even though they didn't share romantic love for one another.

Carter slipped the thin gold band on her finger, sliding it over her knuckle where it settled in the deep groove Robbie's engagement and wedding rings had been this morning. Then Carter placed his ring on her outstretched palm.

She closed her fingers around the jewelry, repeated the magistrate's words and then slipped Carter's wider band on his ring finger. He gave her a reassuring smile before they turned back to the judicial officer.

Carter sure seemed certain now, but when the eggs had slipped from his grip earlier, he'd appeared nervous. Because of his jittery state, she had made small talk on their drive here, which hadn't been hard because Carter was easy to talk with. She had made him laugh about some goat antics from earlier in the day and had appreciated his baritone chuckle that sounded genuine. Over the drive, he appeared to loosen up and forget about his little arthritis incident. She was thankful because she'd been afraid that if they spoke about their concerns, they'd cancel the appointment and Addie wouldn't get the insurance plan she needed. Emma was hesitant to give Carter an easy way out, since she was downright desperate to get her daughter's medicine covered.

"I now pronounce you husband and wife," the magistrate announced. "What God has joined together, let no man put asunder."

Even though she knew they were right with God, uncertainty about their situation swirled in her gut. She glanced at Carter, dapper in his Sunday best. Suddenly, he looked about as nervous as she felt. Hopefully, their unease was temporary.

Emma's gaze met the magistrate's warm and encouraging face as he closed the Bible in his hands and pressed it to his chest.

"You may kiss your bride," the judicial officer said.

Her heart jumped into her throat. She and Carter hadn't talked about this part. They had decided not to hold hands during the vows, choosing instead to focus on the man in front of them. How had they not foreseen this moment and planned accordingly?

The magistrate nodded to them as if to say, *Let's get on with it.*

She turned to Carter as anxiety built in her chest.

The alarm on his face was almost comical. She gave him a small smile. Should she say something? Maybe tell the magistrate that this wasn't a real marriage or maybe that—

Carter leaned in as though he was going to kiss her. Her pulse raced while she remained frozen in place, unsure what she should do to stop him. Instead, he veered a little left and brushed his soft lips against her cheek and then quickly returned to his safe spot across from her.

Relief left her weak at the knees. Why had she worried? She swallowed the emotional lump in her throat. Carter was such a gentleman, of course he'd solve the problem they'd found themselves in.

After the ceremony concluded, they made their way out of the courtroom.

"Maybe we should have had Pastor Tony marry us," Carter whispered as they stepped onto the shiny tiled hallway with even taller ceilings.

She gave a stern shake of her head. "Then everyone and their mother in Serenity would know we were married." Though it wouldn't be long before everyone knew. Would people think ill of her for marrying only six months after Robbie's death? Or would they understand the predicament she'd been in with Addie's medicine? She hoped their church family would give them grace. Though a marriage of convenience for her children was worth any unpleasant encounters with townspeople.

"Good point." His poise gave her the assurance she needed right now.

She couldn't believe that after today, she and the triplets would be grafted into the McCaw family. As someone who'd grown up in foster care, she hadn't had many close friends. Who was she kidding? Robbie had been her only close friend, and she still wasn't sure how to do life without him.

"Can I call you 'Wifey'?" Carter winked as he opened the large glass door and they exited the building.

She chuckled at his attempt to bring some lighthearted humor into a serious moment, one of the many things she appreciated about her friend. "If you want to live, you won't," she jested back. Her heels tapped along the concrete sidewalk. She thanked God for providing her amazing Robbie and gracing them with triplets. Now she had Carter. Just his presence made her relax. Maybe for the first time since she had lost Robbie.

Carter opened the passenger-side door of his luxury sedan and she slid onto the comfortable leather seat, unease over their marriage settling in.

She still loved Robbie, probably always would. But now she was married to someone other than her first love and it wasn't a good feeling.

As she considered her new situation, her heart pummeled her ribs. She smoothed her new sundress with her sweaty palms as Carter settled beside her. Having insurance for Addie's medication was one thing, but with Carter's new role in the triplets' lives, she couldn't help but worry over whether they'd forget their father altogether.

Chapter Four

Carter's mandatory meeting ended right before lunch the following day, and he clicked off his computer. Now he was ready to focus on Emma, the triplets and the goat farm for a few hours. When he'd moved into the RV, he'd realized that living on the property would allow him to spend more time with the triplets and also take a small load off Emma by helping with some of her chores. He rubbed the back of his neck. As long as he didn't do anything stupid like lose the grip on eggs like he had yesterday morning. That had been embarrassing. He'd been sure Emma would call off the wedding. But she hadn't.

When he'd opened his eyes this morning and felt the metal band around his ring finger, the nervousness that had kept him up half the night returned. Then, memories of the triplets racing around the backyard after the wedding ceremony yesterday played in his mind, and it hit him. He was responsible for a family now. It was one thing to put Emma and the triplets on his medical insurance, but to be an instant father? What had he been thinking?

He leaned back in his comfortable office chair and dragged his fingers over the stubble lining his jaw. His mind had been on Emma and trying to resolve her medical insurance problem. Since she had trust issues, it made sense she wouldn't marry some random guy just because he was healthier than Carter. But this marriage arrangement felt so rushed it made his head spin. He still had doubts about being a good father and partner to Emma.

He shook off the negative thoughts and stepped out of the RV door right as Esther drove up to give Emma a reprieve.

Earlier, when he'd gone into the house for a cup of coffee, the triplets had just woken and Addie had been cranky, so Carter had offered to feed the goats to give Emma time to pacify the little girl. *See, helpful*, and Emma had appreciated his thoughtfulness.

His chest puffed out at the memory. With Esther here, Emma would be heading over to the goat pens and Carter wanted to assist her in any way he could.

When Robbie and Emma had moved here with their plan that included goats and chickens for now, he'd been a little jealous because his friend had come up with an alternative rancher role that Carter felt was within his reach. Now, that enticing opportunity dangled like a carrot in front of him. He strode over to the side of the house where they kept their shoes and placed the Stetson Emma had given him as a wedding present on his head.

Emma eyed him as he kicked off his sneakers. "I don't need any help, but Esther might," she stated.

He shrugged, acting as though her rejection hadn't stung. "I'd like to know more about the goat farm and what I can do to lend a hand." Whether she liked it or not, part of being her husband meant he was her helpmate. And he had taken his vows seriously.

At his words, her shoulders crumpled. "It's hard to have someone other than Robbie work with me."

"Oh, I—"

Before he could finish, she turned and strode to the goat yard while he struggled to get his muck shoes on, grimacing at the arthritic pain in his hips that made him feel like an old man. At least Emma wasn't by his side to see his weakness.

He made his way toward the goats. Emma had paused halfway between the house and the pen, thumbs flying on her phone. She had to understand he had no intention of taking Robbie's place.

"Sorry." She looked over her shoulder. "A customer wants goat milk and is asking for the best time to stop by," she said, then pocketed her phone and joined him, their boots crunching over the gravel drive. She hurried to the goats, the bleating noises growing as they neared.

"Oh no," she exclaimed and then rushed over to the girl's pen. He followed, propping his foot on the split-fence rail, the zip-tied chicken wire keeping the toe of his muck boot from going too far.

She squatted down, running her hands over the back of a couple of the goats. One looked hunched over and in pain. Another was grinding her teeth. And the smell. He wrinkled his nose and took a step back. Oof, their pen didn't usually have an overwhelming odor.

Emma looked up at him. "Dolly, Grace

and Jewel are all sick." Her features were full of angst.

"What can I do?"

She glanced at their feed bins. "They didn't finish their breakfast. And goats never leave food."

Emma narrowed her eyes at him and ran to the feed barrel. "The grain is moldy! Oh my, they probably have food poisoning." She plopped the lid down and turned. "How did you not notice the mold when you fed them this morning?"

He eyed Dolly, Grace and Jewel, who were obviously uncomfortable. His gut clenched. How had he overlooked mold, of all things? That should have been obvious.

"I… I don't know. I'm so sorry." He'd been trying to lend a hand by feeding the goats so Emma could focus on Addie's needs, but instead these girls were sick because of him.

Worse yet, he'd let Emma down.

"Ugh, I'm sorry for overreacting," she

said. A softness had returned to her voice. "You were only trying to help earlier and I appreciate the extra set of hands. The moldy grain could have happened to anyone, me included. Likely, the grain you fed the girls was slightly damp when you scooped it, not moldy."

The phone in her back pocket beeped. She pulled out the device and studied it.

He gazed at the ground and contemplated his dusty boots, thankful for the quick apology but wondering if it might be wiser to go back to the playroom instead of staying to help.

Pastor Tony's words from the other day were still in his head and he might never forget them.

Carter chose to stay.

An hour later, he wiped his brow, satisfied with their hard work and the laughs they'd shared. He had woken up this morning with the plan to take some of Emma's burdens off her shoulders. He hoped he had been successful.

On their way back to the house, Emma laid a hand on his arm, a smile lighting her pretty face as though the mold was gone from her mind. She might be able to forget the situation, but he wasn't sure he could forgive himself for the slip up.

"Thank you, Carter. I appreciate your hard work. We got more than I expected checked off my to-do list."

He nodded, thankful they had proven they could work well together and have fun.

On the porch, he kicked off his muck boots and let himself into the kitchen, securing the door behind him. His knees were screaming at him for all the bending and twisting the chores had required, but it had been worth it to have Emma appreciate his hard work.

Giggles and soft talking greeted him, as though Esther were reading a book to the triplets. Just hearing the children's noises made Carter grin. He washed his hands and forearms and then took a few pain reliever tablets before checking on the sweetest three-year-olds he'd ever met.

"Unkie C," Addie screeched when she saw Carter. "Up, up." The girl extended her arms out.

Even though Carter's hands were sore from the chores, he picked up the little girl. She nuzzled her head into his shoulder and rubbed her eyes. It was a little early for them to go down for a nap, but perhaps Addie hadn't slept well last night. He hugged her tight as he made his way over to a rocker.

Esther closed the book and Cassie crawled off the couch. The room appeared fairly picked up, as if Esther had tried to put away toys as they were abandoned.

"So, how's married life?"

Carter gasped. People knew they were married? If so, did they know it was a marriage of convenience or were they assuming it was real? He settled the now-sleeping Addie on a crib mattress on the floor that Emma used for sudden naps during the day.

"Um, good, I guess," he said to the wall of windows, embarrassed to turn around and look the woman in the eye.

"I'm back," Emma stated as she slipped through the tall baby gate. "How were they for you?"

"Very good. Addie was sleepy. She finally nodded off when Daddy got here. Cassie has been in a mood, but reading seemed to calm her. Mikey has been himself."

Daddy. Did Esther just call him *Daddy*?

He turned from the bank of windows and Mikey lunged at him as if to scare him.

Carter bit back a laugh at the little boy's antics and jumped back as though frightened. Mikey laughed and he joined in. Ignoring his aching hands, he lifted the child, then threw him in the air a few inches. Mikey's sudden giggle warmed his heart. He was definitely getting the better end of the marriage bargain.

Movement caught his attention as he spotted Esther leaving. He gave her a thankful nod.

"Again, again," Mikey said from above. Even though Carter's hands throbbed, he threw him one more time. After this, he'd have to put the toddler down and get an ice pack to hold for some relief.

Right as he caught Mikey, the boy's face grew serious, and he vomited. Carter leaned away, but still, the stinky contents of his stomach landed all over Carter's shirt. Some clung to his hair. Carter set the boy on the ground and used a nearby paper towel to wipe the liquid off Mikey's sad face.

He never should have roughhoused with the boy. He hadn't meant for this to happen.

Emma rushed over and threw the roll of towels at Carter. "You're going to want to shower and change quickly or that stench will be impossible to wash away," she snapped.

He headed for the kitchen. He knew when he was being dismissed.

"Mikey's burning up," Emma said.

He looked back and she was feeling Mikey's forehead. He rushed over to Addie. As he neared, he could see she was flushed. He felt her forehead with the back of his hand. "Addie's warm, too."

Emma caught his gaze, a worried look in her eyes. "I heard the flu was going around. Maybe they picked up germs in the church nursery?" She shook her head. "Go shower. I mean it, Carter, that stuff will sink into your skin if you aren't careful." Then she grinned and the corners or her eyes crinkled.

Relief washed over him because she wasn't dismissing him, she was teaching him a parenting lesson.

"I'll be back soon," he said.

"You better be." She chuckled and her eyes twinkled in merriment. Emma's low laugh flowed over him, intriguing him. Before he could analyze those surprising thoughts, he rushed back to the RV to freshen up.

Maybe she had forgiven him for the moldy grain, but he needed to watch his steps. Otherwise, this marriage of convenience would become awkward. And he'd promised Robbie to watch after Emma, not upset her.

Emma startled awake at the sound of the gate clicking shut. She checked and all three children were still sleeping: Addie sound asleep on her chest, Cassie on the mattress on the floor and Mikey squished between her and the couch back. So what had made that noise?

The sun had risen since she'd last wiped off a mouth or changed yucky clothing or put a watered-down-juice sippy cup together. All of their fevers had broken in the middle of the night. *Thank You, Lord.*

She'd probably gotten a solid three hours of sleep, which wasn't bad, all considered.

She spotted Carter creeping into the room, smelling like soap, and she smiled, grateful for the man who had weathered the flu storm with her yesterday afternoon and last night.

He pumped his eyebrows at her and came close. Close enough that she could smell his minty breath.

"I fed the chickens and goats," he whispered, "just like you did yesterday. I also freshened everyone's water." He looked a little nervous at his statement.

She started to fidget at his words then stopped. She didn't want to wake Addie, but what if he had fed them too much? They could get sick. "Did you get the—"

"I filled the hay racks just like you did."

If Addie wasn't lying on top of her, sound asleep, Emma would rush out to the goat yard to make sure he had done the chores right. She hadn't thought he'd been paying attention yesterday, but apparently he had. He'd taken the initiative to lend a helping hand this morning. Gratitude should fill her heart, not suspicion.

"Thank you, Carter, I appreciate your hard work," she said. His face lit up at the compliment.

She hadn't expected him to be playful. Charming even. Who was this guy and how did she get so fortunate to be matched with him?

She was grateful he'd been there last night to help with the triplets' sickness. Having another set of hands was such a blessing.

When they married, she had assumed Carter would stay in his lane by working his usual nine-to-five and maybe have dinner with them or something. But based on his helpful behavior in the goat yard yesterday, he planned on being hands-on. What if his helpfulness made her and the triplets forget Robbie?

As Carter moved from a crouch to a seated position, the pain that crossed over his features startled her. He quickly smiled to cover up the discomfort from his arthritis and leaned back on his palms with his legs splayed out in front of him. "Now, what can I do?"

His question made her forget about his momentary pain and she immediately flipped into mommy mode as her mind replayed the overnight events. The vomiting, the never-ending sippy cups full of either watered-down Pedialyte or apple juice, the soiled pile of baby blankets the triplets loved.

She made a move to get up, but Carter gently pressed her shoulder back. "Don't wake the little ones," he whispered. "I thought the goal was sleep?" Then he winked at her.

Her stomach flipped at the gesture and she didn't have time to wonder why, because he had a point. She was stuck in this position until Addie and Mikey wakened.

"If you wouldn't mind, load the dishwasher with the sick buckets and all the sippy cups we used while they had a fever and run it on the long cycle. Maybe run that basket of soiled blankets in the washer on hot-hot." She hated to ask anything of anyone, but the sooner those tasks were completed, the sooner the day could start. With fever-free triplets, today would probably be busy.

"Done." He gave her a sly grin, as though proud of himself for thinking ahead and doing those tasks without being asked. He should be, because she was shocked. "I also wiped down all surfaces with disinfecting wipes. My mother used to do that after a sickness ran through the family."

His ability to figure out what needed to be done and take the initiative floored her. "Thank you," she whispered. A lump formed in her throat at the thoughtfulness of his actions.

"I know you probably need to get to work, so thanks for all your help." She didn't mean to be so forward, but he was sitting so close. When she'd accepted his marriage of convenience, she hadn't expected he'd be hanging around so much. Of course, when he'd had a satellite internet service installed on the property because much of the time he planned to work from the RV in his accounting role, she should have figured that out.

"Didn't I tell you I took the week off? I mean other than that mandatory meeting yesterday."

That's right, she'd forgotten. Must be the lack of sleep. Regardless, she didn't want to burden him with becoming needy or anything. He had his own life.

He ran his hand along Addie's hair. The overwhelming love he had for Addie melted her heart. To have a second parent helping raise the triplets was an enormous benefit if she could just get over her fear of sullying Robbie's memory.

Carter gave an obvious swallow. Her chest warmed with how much he cared for her children. He'd given up a lot to become her husband and a sudden father to three. Now he'd proven he could handle both roles even though he'd thought his early onset arthritis would slow him down.

"Oh, have you added us to your insurance? I need to pick up Addie's prescription within the next few days." She'd already put the first two purchases on her credit card and had no hope of paying the astronomical balance off in the near future. Just making the minimum payments was a stretch.

He flinched as though someone had hit him. "Oh no, I totally forgot. I'm so sorry. I'll do that right now." He struggled to stand and stiffly left the room as though his arthritis were bothering him.

Her temples throbbed that he hadn't handled the issue, but she couldn't be too hard on him. He'd spent the night helping with three sick kids, handled the morning goat feeding and had cleaned up before she could ask. But if he didn't enroll them soon, she'd have to pay out of pocket for Addie's medicine again. And her credit card was almost maxed out.

The next morning, Carter entered the kitchen and Emma threw her hand over her chest as though startled. Cassie continued to screech on her mother's hip.

"I'm sorry. I should have knocked," he said. Why did she always seem surprised by his presence? He lived here. He selected a mug from the cabinet and poured a steaming coffee.

"Oh no, you don't need to knock," she said through Cassie's wails.

Except her sharp tone and wide eyes begged to differ. Seemed like coming into the house was not fine at all. Where'd she expect him to get something to drink or eat?

He poured his coffee and recalled how she'd asked him, right before their vows at the justice of the peace, if he was sure. He'd confidently told her yes, but he was anything but sure. Maybe marriage was like that?

Cassie continued to screech like a cat was being tortured, so he took the kitchen dishtowel and lifted it to cover his face. "Where's Unkie C?" he said in a singsong voice. Cassie's howl slowed as though she were interested in Carter's game, while Emma continued to pour milk into three sippy cups.

Carter dropped the towel and said, "Here I am."

Cassie paused her crying to stare at him. Emma twisted the tops on the cups while Carter repeated the process and, just like that, the unhappy three-year-old giggled.

He opened the fridge for creamer and saw the delectable chocolate mousse from last night. "Hey, you should sell your mousse in the family store."

"You think?"

"Absolutely, it's delicious. With the mousse, you wouldn't have to share any of the profit with a third party, like you do with the baker from Love Valley."

He turned back to his coffee and noticed Emma sway. He rushed over and took Cassie from her arms. Up close, Emma looked flushed and sweaty.

"How about you sit down for a minute?" He took her elbow and led her into the playroom where Mikey vroomed Matchbox cars and Addie tucked a baby doll into a carriage. He set Cassie down, who promptly rushed over to the baby dolls and grabbed her favorite by the neck.

Emma settled on the couch and immediately slouched on the throw pillow.

"Maybe you should go back to bed?"

Emma straightened. "No, I have too much to do today." But as her eyes closed, he wondered if she was about to fall asleep. He pulled up a poof and sat down in front of her. Man, she was really flushed. Did she have a fever? Oh no, maybe she had picked up the triplets' virus.

Her eyes opened and she gazed at him, looking exhausted and not well.

If she refused to go to her bedroom and rest, then he'd have to get her to-do list and help out.

"I have to get Addie's prescription," she whispered.

"I've added all of you to my insurance and gotten a confirmation, so the prescription should be covered. I can pick it up for you."

Emma's brow wrinkled and a tear glistened down her cheek. "Thank you. That'd be good." She shivered.

He snagged a blanket off the stack and covered her. She snuggled in.

He went to the kitchen and grabbed the three milks, giving one to each of the triplets. When they finished their drinks, he rinsed out the cups and put them in the dishwasher. Noticing his untouched coffee, he downed it and contemplated the day. Since he'd taken the rest of the week off from work, he didn't need to contact anyone from the office. He filled a large tumbler with ginger ale and twirled the lid and straw on. Filled another tumbler with the electrolyte drink they'd used for the children, but didn't dilute it.

When he returned, Emma's eyes were closed, but she didn't look peaceful. Not at all. His heart squeezed that she'd become ill. *Lord, take her illness and give it to me. I'd rather be the one not feeling well.*

Her eyes fluttered open and he offered the ginger ale and electrolytes drink. She took a sip of the ginger ale and then slipped it onto the floor beside the couch. He grabbed the poof and smashed it against the couch right next to her hand, making an ad hoc table. Then he put the two drinks and a tissue box within easy reach.

He did his best to keep the triplets quiet in the playroom. Should he help Emma to her bed so she could get a more restful sleep? He wasn't sure what to do. Every once in a while, she'd grab one of the two drinks and take a few sips, or tug the fuzzy blanket higher and roll over.

The only thing she'd asked him to do was pick up the prescription. But while she was asleep, he needed to watch the children. Eventually, he took them outdoors to play and then fed them a quick lunch. His mother stopped by with some soup for Emma but had to rush back to the Triple C Ranch, where she lived and worked, for her summer camp.

While he was putting the triplets down for their afternoon nap, Emma came into the bedroom as he was finishing the last story. She grinned at him when the children rushed to her. Emma hugged each of them and then settled them in their beds for their nap.

When she came out of the room, he asked how she was feeling.

"Much better. I can't believe I was out for so long."

"My mom brought over some homemade chicken soup a little while ago. It's in the Crock-Pot on warm. Want some?"

"Oh, wow, that sounds yummy." She followed him into the kitchen, moving much slower than usual. She settled in a chair and then sagged as though sapped of energy.

He ladled the soup into a country-blue stoneware bowl and brought it to her along with a spoon and napkin.

"Join me?" she asked.

"I ate with the triplets. Grilled cheese." He made a face. "It's one of the few things I know how to make."

"And I'm grateful." She tasted the soup. "This hits the spot. Thank you for caring for the children for so long."

Oh, if she'd only seen how much he'd looked like an old man today. When he'd made the mistake of kneeling to fix the sunshade on Cassie's baby doll pram, his knees had screamed in revolt. Then, after sitting at Mikey's train table for an extended period, it had taken him several excruciating minutes to stand. Later on, when he was crouching down to assess and then kiss Addie's elbow, he'd had to hold back the hiss on his lips from the pain radiating from his knees.

"Want me to pick up that prescription now or let you—"

"I thought you already took care of it," she cut him off, eyes wide. She seemed panicked about refilling Addie's biologics medicine, then her shoulders slumped. "Of course, I was asleep and you couldn't leave the triplets." She glanced at the wall clock. "I could probably get to the pharmacy before it closes."

He stood, his knees aching at the overuse these past six hours. "No, Emma, you're too weak. I'll go." A rush of dread squeezed his chest because he didn't want to disappoint her.

"Thank you, Carter. I appreciate it," she said, but he didn't turn around. He just lifted a hand in acknowledgement and walked to the door as quick as his sore legs could carry him. He grabbed his wallet and keys, then headed for the drugstore.

He should have thought to have a sister-in-law or one of his siblings come over to watch the children while Emma was napping. Then the prescription would have been at the house when Emma woke up.

When they'd entered this marriage bargain, he'd had a feeling he'd fall short and not be able to juggle all the normal chores of being a good father.

His heart constricted that he might be right.

Chapter Five

After breakfast the next morning, Emma herded the triplets into the playroom and wondered where Carter was. She shook off the question. After he'd been so sweet to care for her yesterday and spent the day on daddy duty, he deserved a morning to sleep in. Except, she had missed him during morning chores. She could always count on him to make her laugh.

Addie came over, climbed in her lap and stuck her thumb in her mouth. Automatically, Emma felt her forehead. No obvious fever. Maybe she was just a little sleepy. That illness had affected Addie worse than the others. But at least she wasn't complaining about sore joints.

Then Emma recalled the biologics medicine Carter had picked up yesterday. A ten-dollar copay. She grinned right as Addie slid off her lap and headed toward the baby dolls.

Her phone dinged with a text message from Carter.

Can you bring some water and maybe a ginger ale?

Oh no. Her heart sank. He'd picked up the virus, too. Yesterday, he'd been her strength when she'd been weak. Today, it was her turn to be strong for him. But how could she bring him things and care for the children at the same time?

"Yoo-hoo, I come bearing caffeine," Autumn called as the front door clicked behind her.

"Stop right there," Emma said as Autumn's sandal-clad foot hung over the gate.

"The triplets had some bug a few days ago. I was sick yesterday and now, Carter has it. So you might not want to come in here and breathe these germs."

Autumn stepped into the room anyway and lifted a sweating iced-coffee drink. "For you, madam. How about we go to the backyard for our chat? No germs in fresh air." So, Autumn went outside with the drinks and Emma got everyone's shoes on and joined her with the triplets.

"I need to bring supplies to Carter, do you mind?" Emma nodded at the children.

"Go right ahead."

Emma grabbed a cute basket and gathered some water bottles, ginger ale and some of those electrolytes drinks they'd watered down for the children. She tossed in a box of tissues and a sleeve of saltine crackers and rushed to the RV.

He was splayed out on the couch, feet hanging over the edge of the pint-sized furniture, eyes closed. She hadn't thought much about him living in here. This was more like a place to spend a night, not the next several months.

She swiveled the huge rolling chair that his brothers had delivered yesterday and placed the basket on it. Everything Carter needed was within reach. He appeared to be sleeping, so she turned to go.

"Don't leave," Carter croaked then licked his dry lips.

Her gut clenched that she and the triplets had given him this bug. "I'm right here."

He looked at the basket. "Fancy. And to think I just stacked drinks on that poof next to the couch and deserted you."

"All I wanted yesterday was sleep. You did good." Even though he had a fever and probably felt all achy, he managed a crooked smile. "You don't seem sleepy."

"I dropped here last night and haven't moved since."

With no blanket? She reached under the couch and pulled out a couple of blankets from the storage compartment. "You must have been chilled." He shrugged.

Even though it was the middle of June and there was no air-conditioning in the RV, he was shivering. Yesterday, when she'd been sick, she'd felt like she was in a walk-in freezer until her fever had broken.

She lay the blanket on top of him. He pulled it up to his chin, his eyelids briefly closing as though he enjoyed the warmth of the cotton even though it was in the eighties already today. She tossed the other two blankets near his feet, where he could easily reach them.

"Wish I knew that cubby with the blankets was there last night." His eyes sparkled with thankfulness, though they were still a little glassy.

"Listen, Carter, the offer of the guest room still stands. It'd be much more comfortable—"

"No," Carter interrupted. Something flashed over his face, but she couldn't read it. "I like this place." He chuckled, but she wondered why he insisted on living in the

RV. Sure, it'd be weird to have him in the house, but they were married.

She stood. She couldn't change his mind, especially when he wasn't feeling well. "Autumn's here. I don't want to leave her too long with the kids."

"Of course. Go ahead. Thanks for the swanky drinks."

"I'll check in on you when the children go down for their nap." She could tell the blanket had made him sleepy. He'd probably take a nice nap of his own as soon as she left.

After the triplets were asleep for their afternoon nap, she brought the pot she had reheated his mother's chicken soup in to the RV, making sure the volume of the baby monitor app on her phone was turned to high.

When she stepped into the RV, Carter swung his legs to the ground.

"Feeling better?"

He lifted his head to peer into the pot. "Is that soup I smell?"

She smiled. "You are feeling better if this smells good to you." She found a bowl and spoon while he settled at the tiny table and dove into the soup like he hadn't eaten in days. She was grateful he seemed better because she felt a little responsible. If he hadn't been helping her with the triplets, he never would have caught this illness.

At the first bite, his eyes rolled back in his head. "This tastes so good. Thank you."

"Carter, it's the least I could do since it's my fault you got sick." She grimaced. "Toddlers are the most dangerous biowarfare known to parents." He'd been so kind to her yesterday that she wanted to do what she could to ease his burdens right now.

"That's for sure." He took another sip and the color seemed to return to his cheeks. "It isn't your fault. I wanted to help." He finished the bowl and pushed it away.

"More?" she asked.

He shook his head. "I'm good for now.

But I was thinking about your family store earlier and I have an idea for an online presence." Excitement laced his tone. "All those items from local friends aren't moving because they've already sold their maximum here in Serenity. But an online store would open up a new and larger customer base."

She frowned. "Sounds like a lot of work for you just to help some older people who don't know how to navigate the internet."

"Once we set it up, keeping the inventory updated won't require much effort. Like you said, it helps people who aren't familiar with creating an online presence sell their wares to a larger market. Since you'll own the store, you'll get the commission, just like the deal you have here." He shifted his legs to get more comfortable and a hint of discomfort crossed over his face. She wanted to suggest that he move back to the couch, but held her tongue.

"I feel funny taking a cut when products sell." But back when the ladies had asked her to display their quilts, bead bracelets and earrings, they'd insisted. Yet she'd only sold a couple pairs of earrings. Her big sellers were the goat milk, desserts, meat and the jarred relishes, jams and pickles.

"You shouldn't. That's how it's done."

Adrenaline flooded her system at the thought of her family store generating passive income. "I love that idea. Could you list the quilts, too?" She felt bad that she'd had those four quilts hanging on a ladder rack for over a year. Other than dusting them, no one had shown any interest in them. But the ladies in town had insisted she keep them until they sold. Had even told her they had lots more where they'd come from.

He grinned and the dimple on his left cheek appeared, drawing her gaze to him. Yes, he was a handsome man, but more importantly, he was sweet, considerate and selfless. Emma admired those qualities. Perhaps more than she'd like to admit.

"They'll be a big-ticket item," he said. "The shipping cost would be paid by the buyer. And the relishes, jams and pickles might generate some interest online as well."

"Wow, Carter, that's a great idea. I'm excited to see where this will lead." But then she remembered her failure at numbers. This venture would be one more way that her dyscalculia would become obvious to those around her.

"Once I create the online presence, you can reach out to the others so we can list any other items they might have as well." He sighed. "Okay. Maybe I'm not all better. I think I'm going to lie down again."

She didn't want to leave because she enjoyed talking with him. She hadn't realized how much she missed having someone around. Carter was fun and engaging. As he settled on the couch, he groaned. She eyed him, disappointed, but she understood he needed his rest.

She made sure he had everything he

needed, then reluctantly returned to the house. Spying the inviting rocker on the front porch, she decided to take a moment to get some fresh air and mull over the exciting online store possibility.

She settled, set the chair in motion and let her imagination run wild. Passive income was exactly what she needed, what with the hospital bill she'd just negotiated as well as that debt on her credit card from the first two months of Addie's prescriptions.

Maybe an online store would allow her to pay off her debts a little quicker. She smiled as hope thrummed through her core. That would be an unexpected, yet welcome, blessing.

Sunday after church, they had lunch and then Emma put the triplets down for their nap. While the afternoon sun shined bright through the window above the sink, Carter cleaned up the kitchen. His chest swelled at all the congratulatory wishes they'd received at church. Everyone had been encouraging, and no one had appeared shocked by his and Emma's quick nuptials.

"I can't believe the dogs will be here in a few minutes," Emma said as she entered the kitchen. "Thanks for all this." She swept her hand around the now-cleaned-up kitchen.

"It's the least I could do after you were so attentive when I was sick." His heart had hitched each time she'd knocked and then opened the RV door. Especially the times when she was able to stay for a bit to chat. He hadn't realized how much he enjoyed her company.

"I'll be outside," she said and turned to leave.

He dried his hands and joined her as she slid on her muck boots. He hurried after her, slowing when he got to the steps. He took them one at a time, grimacing at the arthritic pain in his hips that made him feel much older than he was.

"Oh, Carter, I'm so sorry about that." Her brow scrunched up with concern for his discomfort.

Heat flamed his face that she'd noticed his weakness. Not that she didn't already know about his illness, but he preferred to gloss over it as much as possible.

He schooled his features, kicking himself for advertising obvious distress on his face, and slid on his Stetson that no longer looked new. "It's nothing."

"No, Carter, it's something. Hopefully, changing to the anti-inflammatory diet will help you." They made their way toward the goat pen, their boots crunching over the gravel drive.

While he'd been holed up in the RV with the flu, she had researched arthritis. Mostly because she'd wanted to make sure she was doing everything she needed for Addie. In her research, she'd discovered that an anti-inflammatory diet could help many types of arthritis. So she'd switched their diet a couple of days ago. Hopefully, he'd notice a difference soon.

Before they reached the pens, he heard a vehicle approaching. He turned his head just as Autumn's dusty minivan pulled up.

He exchanged a jubilant glance with Emma and their gazes tangled for a moment. What was that?

"The dogs are here," she said, breaking the moment as heat rose in her cheeks. They'd both been looking forward to the start of having guard dogs on the property. She rushed over to the minivan, Carter close behind.

The sooner the dogs got settled, the sooner they'd be ready to protect the herd. His steps faltered. Except, he'd been enjoying living on Jubilee Farm. Playing Daddy to the triplets, helping with the herd and spending time with Emma.

"Here they are," Autumn said as she opened her door. Her husband, Wyatt, got out the passenger door. "Are you guys ready?"

They followed his sister to the back of her van. Though it had been uncomfortable, he'd been honest with his parents and siblings about the reason he and Emma had married. Thankfully, they all appeared understanding. His sister opened the door and released the two Great Pyrenees, who were much larger than he had expected.

"They are gorgeous." Carter sank his fingers into their thick, white fur. It kind of felt like a blanket.

"The children will want to ride them." Emma giggled.

"Since they are about the size of a miniature pony, they probably will." Autumn closed the van doors while the dogs sat at attention, watching her.

"Like we've told you," Wyatt said, "they aren't ready to guard just yet, but we want them to live on the farm and get used to you guys and the goats and everything."

"Thank you for finding them for us," Emma said to her brother-in-law. It was a blessing to have someone connected to the dog community in the family."

"Happy to," Wyatt said. "I'm turning this project over to Autumn. She can take over from here."

Autumn's cheeks pinked at her husband's confidence in her. "Yes, I'll come over twice a week, but I'll need the two of you to practice what I teach, okay?"

He and Emma nodded. They were one step closer to not having a coyote problem anymore.

"Let's introduce these guys to the goats. We'll keep the fence between them for a couple of days. By the way, this is Bear." Autumn pointed to the bigger one. "And this one's Roxy."

Carter leaned over to pet Bear and Roxy, thankful they hadn't arrived fully trained. These Great Pyrenees were going to buy him a little more time to enjoy living on Jubilee Farm.

They agreed on a training schedule that would work with all of them before Autumn and Wyatt drove off, back toward the Triple C.

Another truck arrived.

Emma turned and waved. "That's Silas Murray, to replenish the beef supply." She strode over to the vehicle that had turned around and now was backing up toward the family store door. Carter followed, figuring he could help.

They unloaded the collapsible crates full of rib eye steaks and ground beef, the two items Emma had run out of. Silas got the beef in the door, told Emma he'd be back for the crates later on and then took off.

Emma thanked him and waved. "I've never met a more introverted person than Mr. Murray."

"Probably why he approached you about selling to customers, so he wouldn't have to." A smile tugged at her ruby lips. Mr. Murray was a cranky older man, but she was still so kind to him. Her sweet innocence appealed to Carter. Maybe because it offset his cynical nature. "Want me to hand—"

"Nope. I have it. I like to organize all the beef in stacks, so I can tell when I'm getting low."

From doing her bookkeeping, Carter knew the beef sales were a reason her family store was profitable.

He took in the tiny place that was chockfull of goods. The long table opposite the front door held all the delectable baked goods, with the industrial refrigerator behind. Thankfully, when Robbie had enclosed this shed to create Emma's family store, he'd had the bright idea to set the fridge flush with the wall so Emma would have more interior space. Quilts hung in one corner. Homemade bead bracelets and earrings were on the small table in front of Emma's tiny desk. On the wall opposite the deep freezer Silas Murray had provided were sturdy wooden crates that Emma had stacked to make into shelving units to display the jams, jellies, relishes and pickles. Everything sat on a well-loved, multicolor-braided oval rug. Cramped but homey.

Emma collapsed the first crate, slid it behind the freezer and held out a sheet of paper that Silas had given her. "Can you put this receipt in my tally bin? It's the first drawer in the desk."

He approached the tiny corner desk. Everything in him wanted to organize the life out of this messy desk. Instead, he opened the drawer and shoved the paperwork in. He gritted his teeth at her lack of organization. On the other hand, he handled her bookkeeping for her, and she'd never had an overdue or unpaid bill.

"This drawer is more like an overflowing volcano than a simple tally bin."

She shrugged. "Works for me."

He finagled the overfull drawer closed. Before he turned, his gaze came to rest on the messy surface of the desk. A bill with red block letters caught his eye. He twirled the paper around. The center of the paper had a bold red ink stamp that said "Second Notice." His heart landed in his throat. It was from the hospital where Addie had spent a week in the spring. "What's this?" He turned to her.

She rolled her eyes and took the bill. "It's handled."

His stomach coiled into a tight knot at the thought of her being in financial distress of any kind.

He cocked his head as she stuffed the bill away and then tugged at the roll top portion of the desk, only able to get it about halfway down before giving up.

"I can help, Emma. I have money, you know."

She straightened and her pretty sky-blue eyes flashed in irritation. "I've negotiated payment with them. When you don't have insurance, the dollar amount is simply a suggestion to the patient. Like I said. I've got it handled."

"I can help by making phone calls or discussing the best way to handle the situation. We're partners now." Dealing with the flu running through the family should have shown her that. It had sure impacted his world.

He'd been married almost a week and with each day that had passed, he'd grown more fond of the entire family. Especially Emma.

"I know, and I appreciate that." She moved to the store's door. "It's nothing to worry over." She tried to make her tone light and airy, but Carter wasn't buying it. The more she deflected from that overdue bill made him wonder what exactly she meant by the words *negotiated payment*.

He scuffed a hand over his face. As an accountant and certified financial planner, he knew finances from every angle. Why wouldn't she accept advice from him?

His chest tightened with dread. Maybe more important, why was she being so secretive?

Chapter Six

Carter set Mikey in his booster seat at the table two days later and belted him in. "Getting rid of the toddler table was the smartest decision you've made," he stated, elated to partake in another dinnertime.

Emma belted Addie but said nothing. He glanced at her and noticed that sadness had replaced her upbeat demeanor from a few moments ago. He narrowed his eyes at her, what'd he say?

"I'm not sure I had a choice," she forced a chuckle. "You found a donated table and chairs and had a buyer for the toddler table before I said yes."

"But I let you decide," he pointed out. He'd only been trying to help. Should he have kept out of it?

She gave a small shake of her head. The lighting in the kitchen made her eyes a deep ocean blue color. "That was a technicality. Before you approached me, the deal had already been done." She settled Cassie in her seat then she shot him a look. Grateful? He wasn't sure. All he knew was the sadness was gone, replaced with something he couldn't identify. "I guess I'm glad you pushed me out of my comfort zone or these guys would have been teenagers at that table."

"We not guys. We girls," Addie said, pointing between herself and her sister.

"I know, munchkin." Emma's genuine smile reappeared and she tapped the tip of the girl's nose with the sweet love of a devoted mother.

She turned to the counter and as she passed him, she spoke quietly, as though she didn't want the children to hear. "I always thought moving them out of the toddler table was something Robbie and I would do together." Unshed tears brushed her bottom lashes.

He tunneled his fingers through his hair, but before he could think of something to say, she spoke.

"I'm sorry." She touched his elbow and pulled a face. "It's not you, it's me. When big things happen I remember all over again that Robbie's gone."

He wrapped her in a hug, enjoying her floral smell for a moment. Going through life without the man she thought she'd grow old with must be hard.

He got it because he missed his friend as well, but obviously it was different for Emma.

She gave a contented sigh and released him, then turned to work on prepping the plates. The space was small, so he figured if she wanted help, she'd speak up. The triplets were banging their hands on the wooden tabletop, making a cacophony of noise that would have given him a headache a few weeks ago. Tonight, their chatter and impatience warmed his heart.

"Can you help carry the plates over so the little ones don't revolt?" Emma asked.

They worked as a team, putting dinner in front of the triplets: flakes of grilled salmon, chopped tomatoes from his mother's garden and a small scoop of quinoa. Surprisingly, the children hadn't minded the change in diet. Seemed that whenever one of them liked a food, the others would eat it. Emma told him she thought it was because they were competitive.

He and Emma sat, he prayed, then they all started eating.

"What's for dessert?" Mikey asked around a mouthful of quinoa.

"Blueberries. But only if you finish all the food on your plate," Emma said. Even though she'd been caring for goats and chasing around three-year-old triplets all afternoon, she carried the look well. Almost as though those activities didn't exhaust her. Once again, he couldn't get over that this gorgeous woman was his wife.

"Ask," Addie insisted as she looked up at Carter with those blue eyes she'd inherited from her mother.

Carter loved the tradition he'd started as soon as the toddler table was removed and the booster seats had arrived. "Okay, what was your favorite part of the day?"

Three little hands shot into the air. Another tradition he'd started that he'd learned in his childhood. Take turns. "Addie, I think it is your turn tonight."

She stated that learning how to pump on the belt swing was her favorite. Closely followed by petting Roxie. "She's so soft," she stated.

"She picked mine. That's not fair," Mikey said. He crossed his arms to pout until his mother reminded him that blueberries were the dessert. He eyed her for a moment before gobbling up his food.

"Cassie, what about you, sweetie?"

"I liked it when Bear and Roxy knocked

me down and licked my face," she said. The dogs hadn't knocked her down on purpose. They were sweet, lovable and overwhelmingly large, but he didn't correct her. "I think I'm their favorite."

A chorus of noes rang out. He paused eating to push Mikey's food back to the center with his fork, while Emma did the same with the girls. He and Emma had found a rhythm of working together with the goats and triplets. In the early days of their marriage he never thought he'd get to the point of being helpful rather than a hinderance, but these days he knew she appreciated him.

"Okay, less talking and more eating," Emma stated, then she eyed Carter. "Thanks for your help this morning." She chuckled and he shook his head. The girl goats had done everything under the sun to deny Emma the chance to give them oral medicine to fix their food poisoning issue.

"They were slippery."

"Until you showed up." She giggled and lifted her fingertips in front of her mouth.

"We cornered them together."

Her eyes were lit with humor at the memory. "We are quite the team," she said. Then her smile faded and she looked down to study her nearly empty plate while tugging her lip with her bottom teeth. Had he said something? He ran through their exchange, but it was all about the slippery goats. When her eyes filled with tears and she started blinking them back, he knew something had reminded her of Robbie.

Yes, she and Carter were married and good friends, becoming closer every day, but that didn't change the sting of no longer having Robbie by her side.

The next morning, Emma huddled on the couch in the playroom and hugged her knees to her chest. When her phone pinged with a text, she ignored it. She just wanted to stay holed up right there snuggled with her children and eating junk food. Tomorrow would arrive soon enough.

The triplets were crowded in front of the television, watching a short movie because she was afraid if they got upset about anything that she'd cry right along with them.

July Fourth. Her and Robbie's fifth wedding anniversary.

She turned her head from the glare outside. How dare the sun shine today? Seemed like it should be pouring or stormy. But nope, instead full-on sunshine.

It just didn't seem right. Though five years ago today, it had been sunny as well.

Both orphans, she and Robbie had opted for a simple ceremony. He'd wanted to make it the Fourth, so they'd always be able to celebrate on Independence Day with a fireworks celebration. A tear slid down her cheek. She wiped it away.

Her phone pinged again. Since the movie was almost over, she lifted her phone. Carter.

A happy little jolt buzzed in her stomach at the sight of a text from him, which upset her more. Today was about Robbie.

It's gorgeous outside. Let's take the children to my mother's petting zoo. We can let them "ride" the miniature horses, they'll get a kick out of it.

Maybe tomorrow, she replied.

They'd really love it. And they must be going stir-crazy since you haven't been in the backyard yet today.

She rolled her eyes. She wanted him on the property to help watch over the herd, and it didn't hurt knowing he was around if anything else were to happen. But having him work from the RV every day allowed him to keep an eye on her comings and goings. She had just begun getting used to having him around, but today she just wanted to crawl under a rock.

The volume of the video increased, signaling the end of the show, and she was still unsettled. What was making her feel this way? There was something more going on than just her and Robbie's wedding anniversary. She tried to be content with what she had, just like the devotion she'd read this morning in the Book of Philippians instructed.

The movie ended and Mikey rushed over to her. "Can we go outside? I put on my shoes?" His eyebrows lifted in such hope. If she said no, he'd probably throw his body to the ground and start screaming, which she had no bandwidth for today.

She sighed. She would not be any fun today. The least she could do was accept Carter's gracious invitation so the triplets wouldn't be bored to tears all afternoon.

She shot him a text.

Fine. Meet you at the truck in an hour?

He replied with heart-eye emojis, which only made her tear up again since that had been Robbie's favorite emoji.

She changed the excited triplets out of their pajamas, herself too, and loaded them into her extended-cab truck. She almost grabbed her bag of chocolate and side of kettle potato chips, but resisted and got a snack for the children instead. She dropped a handful of goldfish crackers in the cup part of the organizer attached to the headrest in front of each child. Carter had purchased three, attached them, then had the interior of her truck detailed. Apparently, he wanted neatness when they drove around. It didn't really matter to her. Especially today.

Carter arrived at her side, looking dashing as usual. His prior uniform of dress pants and a polo shirt had slowly morphed into deck shorts and a crisp shirt. Today he sported his Dad to the Power of Three tee, a play on the number three and being a father to triplets that his brother, Ethan, had gifted him on Father's Day. He looked more at home in the updated casual clothing. He wore the Stetson she'd given him for their wedding, which appeared more worn with each wear. It made him look more like a rancher than a businessman. A combination of soap and a woodsy smell joined him. She breathed in his manly aroma.

"Thanks for getting me out of the house," she said around the growing lump in her throat. She didn't deserve Carter.

"My pleasure." He gave her a sweet smile, took the keys and rounded the truck as though he hadn't just saved her sanity.

He got behind the wheel and chatted with the children until they arrived at the Triple C Ranch. His countenance remained cheery, like he knew she didn't want to talk. Did he remember it was her anniversary? No, that wasn't something a guy would remember.

"Mommy, my leg hurts," Addie stated from the back seat. Emma swiveled around, her heart in her throat. What if Addie's symptoms returned in force?

What if the expensive medicine stopped working?

She gently touched her daughter's right knee, the original joint that had started this whole process. "Here?"

Addie shook her head. "No, Mama, here." She pointed to a faint scratch on her thigh. "From the jungle gym."

Relief swooshed through Emma that it was a simple scratch and not her juvenile arthritis. She kissed her fingers and pressed them against the scratch. "All better?"

Addie grinned. "Yes!"

Gratitude swept over Emma that Addie wasn't having arthritis pain right now. She looked over at Carter and they shared a secret celebratory glance that Addie was not complaining about joint pain. The ability to communicate wordlessly filled Emma with delight. She appreciated that Carter had made the sacrifice to marry her for the medical insurance, but she hadn't expected them to develop such a deep relationship. Especially not so quickly.

The wide-open Triple C Ranch spread before her as Carter parked the truck. After they got the children out of the car seats, he touched her arm and appeared concerned. "Is everything okay?" he asked.

"Mmm-hmm," she answered as she rushed after the triplets. "Wait at the gate," she called to them. Thankfully, they slowed and Carter didn't push his point. He was good at not pushing her. Usually.

A few days ago, when Carter had seen the overdue bill, she'd quickly recovered. She had made the call from the family store specifically because she hadn't wanted him to overhear the conversation. She was bewildered by how the bill had ended up on her desk. She was sure she'd tucked it away, safe from prying eyes.

Negotiating a payment schedule had been a challenge with her math disability. She'd recorded the conversation between herself and the hospital administrator and then played it back multiple times to make sure the numbers she'd written in her notebook matched what the lady and she had agreed upon. Maybe she should tell her husband about her dyscalculia. Her stomach twisted. No. There was no reason to bring it up. She had her coping mechanisms.

"Memaw," the three of them said in chorus as they changed their course and ran over to Cora, Carter's mother, who had just stepped onto the porch. She knelt and engulfed them in a hug, a wide grin on her face.

Emma leaned on the petting zoo gate. Smells from the chicken and pigs wafted over. Her heart was full that her children now had the McCaws to call family. Before Robbie had passed, they'd spent time with this family, but she'd always felt like an outsider, even though they'd been kind and inviting. But now that she'd married Carter, something had clicked. She wasn't sure if it was them or her, but now she felt like an integrated part of their family, no longer an outsider. She smiled, thankful for the change in attitude. As a child, this had always been her dream. Now that she and Carter were married, even if something happened to her, her children would grow up with these loud, loving and amazing people.

Carter stepped to her side. "Is everything okay at the family store? I saw you go in there briefly this morning." Worried commas appeared between his eyebrows.

The reminder of her shaky family store income made her sadness over the date disappear. Though Dolly, Grace and Jewel were feeling better and the rest of the herd hadn't gotten sick, Emma had been forced to throw their milk away, and would continue that process until she ended the medication. That had set her profits back a bit and made her nervous about making the next hospital payment on time.

But instead of sharing her financial

woes with him, she focused on her new idea. "I'm thinking of making a variety of simple desserts to sell instead of just the mousse." She scuffed her toe in the dirt.

"That sounds like a great idea. Are you sure you don't have a degree in marketing?"

His encouragement meant so much to her. The appreciation shining in his eyes shouldn't make her feel so good. Tears pricked her eyes. Seemed anything made her emotional today.

The triplets and Cora started their way. The children were squealing about the miniature horses. Telling Cora all about Bear and Roxy and how their mother wouldn't allow them to ride the dogs, even though they were humongous.

Cora greeted her with a welcoming hug. Emma pressed her eyes closed at the affection she so needed today. The woman smelled like she'd been baking sugar cookies. The hug ended much too quickly but the sparkle in Cora's eyes made Emma feel at home.

"You two stay out here and relax," Cora said. "I've got them."

"I'll help," Emma stated.

"No, you won't." Cora placed a palm on her arm. "During camp, I have a dozen at a time. You take a moment to relax."

Cora let the triplets into the gate and closed it behind herself, then she asked them to clasp their hands in front of themselves. She praised them and started a well-rehearsed monologue about each animal in the pen. Once Cora had introduced the animal to them, she allowed the children to pet it. The woman had a commanding, yet loving, way about her.

"Anyway, my idea is to rotate through mousse, cake pops and mini cupcakes, each two days a week. First come, first serve."

"A variety of desserts will skyrocket the family store sales."

She wouldn't correct him about her profits, instead she aimed her attention at the triplets.

Cora finally introduced the children to the miniature ponies and allowed the triplets to run their fingers through the long manes.

"Your family is the best." Emma stated the obvious. Jealous of what he'd grown up with. "This is everything I hungered for as a child—stability, love, peace."

Carter bumped her shoulder. "Maybe you didn't have this. But look at what you're giving your children."

Her lips curved into a smile. Something she didn't think was possible today, but Carter was a special guy with powers to charm.

"While we have a minute without little ears listening in," he started and turned to her, his face serious. "I wanted to address that overdue bill."

She folded her arms in front of her, nervous to be completely honest with him. "I told you. It's been taken care of." What she hadn't told him was that the negotiated payment schedule meant the goat farm and family store could not have any blips for the next four months or she'd run overdue on the hospital payments as well. And she didn't want to think about Addie's first few biologics prescriptions that she'd put on the household credit card knowing she could only afford the minimum monthly payment. Every month the balance grew larger.

Thankfully, the full scope of the debits and credits wouldn't be obvious to him until tax season, when she handed over all the receipts. By next April, Emma planned to have all this debt taken care of so even if Carter realized her financial bind, it'd be too late for him to swoop in and fix things.

"Emma." Carter touched her arm and she almost melted at his caring tone. Oh, how she wanted to lean on him, but she had promised herself not to. "I just want to help."

Before she could open her mouth to divulge her financial woes, Mikey yelled for him.

"Unkie C," the boy shouted in excitement, "you have to see this!"

Carter's eyes brightened as he held up a finger to her and then dashed into the pen to take part in Mikey's excitement.

She was grateful for the interruption. She'd best not share with Carter how she had handled the hospital bill by negotiating the price and then signing up for the six-month payment plan because he'd just pay off her balance. And she didn't want him to do that.

Chapter Seven

Two days later, Emma ran her hand over Prancer's neck to check his skin as the hot July sun beat on her back. When she realized the lump felt the same as it had this morning, her shoulders slumped.

Even after spending the morning investigating online and in her little library of research books tucked at the top of a built-in-bookshelf in the corner of the playroom, she had no clue what Prancer's problem was. As the day wore on, she'd become frustrated because she was usually spot on with diagnosing goat issues.

She sucked in a deep breath of fresh hay

and the outside breeze while toying with her limited choices.

Seemed her only option was to leave a message with the town veterinarian. Her heart sank because, like most veterinarians, Doc Earl wasn't fond of working with goats. Usually, she researched and contacted him with specific symptoms, along with her diagnosis and the medication she needed. The veterinarian was happy to leave what she needed at the front desk for her to pick up. But maybe this time he'd be willing to drop by and take a look. She stepped over the straw-covered space, slid out of the buck's pen and shot Doc Earl a 9-1-1 text about Prancer, hoping he'd stop by before dinner.

She spotted Carter coming toward her. Passing by the dogs, he leaned down and petted Bear and Roxy. She smiled at their recent additions, even loving their names. At least something was going right.

"It might take a few months," she said as she closed the distance between them, "but these guys seem to have the right disposition to guard our herd."

She quickly glanced at Carter, who was focused on the dogs at the moment. Had she just said *our*? She shook her head. She should have said *mine*. She rolled her eyes, but she couldn't take it back now. That would offend him, and rightly so. He had done so much for her and the triplets, as well as for the herd and the farm. But this herd had started out as Robbie's dream. Sure, she'd had to take over when Robbie began working full-time and then gotten sick, but she had always considered the herd Robbie's. Now she found that sharing ownership, even in words, was painful.

"I agree. These dogs are amazing," Carter said as he stood. If he had noticed her plural pronoun, he'd chosen not to say anything.

She grappled with the confusing emotions he seemed to evoke ever since the July Fourth fireworks display. He was so good-looking, especially when he wore his Stetson. There was something about the cowboy hat that made him into a more confident man. And she liked that.

Add that he clearly cared for her and the children, and the herd if she were being honest. He spent a good chunk of his time helping her and asking for nothing in return.

His eyebrows wrinkled together in that cute trait he had for when he was worried. He held her gaze an instant longer and a little jolt of pleasure shot through her. She took a step back, displeased by her reaction. That ping of attraction made her feel like she was dishonoring Robbie, and she couldn't have that.

"What's wrong?" His chocolate-brown eyes roamed her features as though he could figure out the problem through guesswork. The last thing she wanted was for him to surmise she might have feelings for him. Most of the time, she appreciated that Carter could read her like an open book. This was not one of those times.

That's when she remembered the reason she was out here—Prancer. Right now, she was uneasy about the buck's unexplainable illness.

"Prancer has a lump on his neck and I can't figure out what it is."

Carter's gaze dashed to Robbie's prized buck. The first goat they'd purchased. The only goat Robbie had named.

Carter insisted on seeing and feeling the lump. They entered the enclosure and while he prodded Prancer's neck, she was able to talk through all the investigating she'd done, hoping he'd ask a question that would trigger something she hadn't thought of.

"So, I don't see a cut or anything. Maybe a sliver from the fencepost?" Carter took his phone, turned on the flashlight and lit up the lump, just like she had. "Nothing obvious. And it's odd that me messing with the lump isn't bothering him," he mused.

She nodded. Unfortunately, nothing she

hadn't already thought of, but his concern warmed her heart.

She recalled the conversation they'd had about the importance of the herd before they'd married. He had assured her that whatever was important to her was important to him. At the time, she had wondered if he was just giving her lip service but, true to his word, he seemed to really care about the herd and the family store.

"You say he's acting normal," Carter stated. "I mean he's eating and drinking and getting into mischief like usual. That's a good thing, right?"

"True." She closed and secured the gate behind her, and her stomach dipped. Carter's levelheaded thinking was why it was dangerous to get close to him. He was perceptive and thoughtful, which tempted her to lean on him. But growing up as an orphan had taught her not to lean on others.

She noticed his insulated cup, the one he used for cold drinks. "You were looking for more green tea, weren't you?"

He lifted his cup. "I've become addicted. And since it's good for me." He shrugged.

As he followed her back to the house, he gave her an update on the online store that he'd started work on in the evenings. He pressed the code then pushed the front door open wide so she could pass through first.

She was becoming excited about the online store and the passive income it would create.

She took the container of green tea out of the fridge as her mind traveled to the Fourth of July. They'd allowed the children to stay up to watch the town fireworks from the backyard, where they could see the show over a ridge of trees. Of course, all three had fallen asleep well before darkness, so by the time the show had started, it was just her and Carter. Five years ago, she'd married Robbie. Every Fourth of July since, they'd been together and watched the show. Even last year, when Robbie hadn't been feeling good.

This year, she'd forced herself to watch in silence while she mourned her late husband. But then the unexpected had happened. When Carter had commented about the color or pattern of one of the illuminations, she'd conversed with him. Before too long, they'd had a normal conversation and she'd enjoyed their time together.

That night, after they'd parted, guilt had eaten her up. How could she enjoy herself when Robbie was no longer here?

"Mama" emitted from the baby monitor on her phone app and from down the hallway. She and Carter exchanged a look as she handed Carter the filled mug.

"You should go before they see you," she said.

She moved down the hall and opened the bedroom door, assuming Carter had slipped out of the house. She spotted Mikey sitting on his pillow, reading a book. He looked up and reached his arms to her. "Papa C," he said. She glanced behind her and Carter stood there, more handsome than ever. A week ago, Mikey had latched on to the new moniker for Carter, and it hadn't taken long for the girls to follow suit. Now they all called him Papa C and though Emma thought it was cute, part of her worried her children might forget their father.

"You're never getting out of here," she said in a fake whisper. He had to get his hours in at his job and spending time with the children would not accomplish that.

Cassie and Addie rushed to her, clinging to her legs. Emma turned to herd them into the playroom, but Mikey hurried over to Carter, who had moved to the well-used rocker she had in the corner of the triplets' room. Carter lifted Mikey and settled him on a leg.

"Come on Addie, Mikey will share," Carter said.

Addie ran over to him as Emma lifted Cassie and propped her on her hip. Her heart melted at the sight of the children so invested in Carter. And he in them.

His eyes sparkled as they chattered away. His proud smile was something to behold. Wow, he looked good holding her children.

He caught her gaze and beamed. Right then a fluttery sensation bubbled in her stomach and she looked away, but not before guilt over her surprising interest in Carter took over.

Her phone pinged with an incoming text message. She strode to the playroom, settled Cassie in front of the dolls, then pulled her phone from her back pocket, thankful for something to do rather than wonder why she had a sudden attraction to Carter.

I'll try to stop by sometime this week, Doc Earl's response read.

Her feet stumbled at the vague timing.

She sank onto the couch, her thumbs hovered over her phone. Should she stress how urgent this situation was? She read her prior message. The urgency seemed pretty clear from her earlier wording, yet he might not make it out for a week. Her chest tightened at her helplessness.

Carter entered the playroom with Mikey and Addie in tow.

"What is it?" Carter asked, striding over to the couch and settling beside her.

She pushed away the fear growing in her gut and told Carter what Doc Earl had said. "If he and I can't figure out what the problem is, I might lose Robbie's prized buck." She swallowed hard and bit back the emotion rising in her throat. "Which means I won't be able to breed this fall. Which means no baby money come springtime." She was disappointed at how high-pitched her voice had become, but with a hefty credit card debt hanging over her head, she couldn't hide her worry.

"Maybe you just resolved the problem. You can buy another buck."

"They're cheaper in the spring, so I'm waiting."

"I could buy a buck now." He grinned. "Call it a wedding gift."

She opened her mouth to respond but instead waited a moment to formulate a kind response. Though she appreciated that he wanted to help, she was an independent woman and had never accepted financial assistance from anyone before. She didn't want to start now. "That's kind of you, Carter, but I can run this farm with my own money. I don't want to have to rely on anyone." She touched his arm. "I hope you can understand." She'd already leaned on Carter more than enough.

He had only married her so they could have medical insurance. She wasn't about to accept financial help from him as well.

The next afternoon, while his mother watched Cassie and Mikey, he and Emma traveled to the doctor's office with Addie for a follow-up appointment with her pediatric rheumatologist.

As Emma checked them in, Addie settled in a hard green chair, clutching her favorite baby doll, and whined, "How long do we have to stay here, Papa C?"

Carter's chest squeezed at the girl's term of endearment. He wasn't sure he'd ever get over this new name. Papa C. With each utterance, Carter's heart felt like it would burst with pride and love.

"Just a few minutes, sweetie," he said as he ran a hand down her long hair. She responded with a pout. Likely because the hospital stay was fresh in her mind.

Emma came over and settled on the other side of Addie. Her hair was pulled back in a messy bun, highlighting her gorgeous cheekbones. Even though she'd been minding the goats and triplets all morning, she looked stunning in her white frilly blouse coupled with stylish capri pants. Addie climbed into her lap and stuck her thumb in her mouth. Emma put her arms around the girl in a protective manner.

Carter slipped into Addie's now-vacant seat. "It'll be okay," he whispered.

Emma looked at him, her wide eyes full

of concern, and his heart stuttered. She captivated him. The way she handled everything with grace, the everlasting love she held for the triplets and that she was drop-dead gorgeous didn't hurt. He still could not believe this magnificent woman was his wife.

"I hope so," she said. He couldn't believe he was responsible for the family, just like Robbie had been.

Carter stretched his neck, astonished at the seriousness of their marriage bargain. The responsibility made his pulse quicken.

"Is your neck okay?" she asked. His cheeks flamed with embarrassment that she always seemed to see when pain crossed over his face from his arthritis.

"I'm good. Just the long drive into Dallas. The traffic here is crazy." She agreed and went back to cuddling Addie.

He'd actually come to Dallas a few days ago to see a rheumatologist. His primary doctor had diagnosed him at eighteen and Carter had never followed up, simply assuming he'd have to live with the disease. But when Emma had read about treating arthritis with an anti-inflammatory diet, he'd decided to see a specialist. The doctor had taken X-rays and indicated that even though he'd been living with joint pain, the images didn't show joint deterioration. Praise God. The specialist recommended collagen, supplements and physical therapy. While checking out, Carter had ordered the recommended high quality collagen and supplements online and had received them this morning. His first physical therapy appointment was tomorrow. Maybe his diagnosed arthritis would become more livable with the changes. He hoped so.

Before long, Addie was called back. Emma carried her to the nurse as Carter pulled out his phone and settled in for a wait.

"Carter."

He looked up and Emma had her head cocked and was waving at him to join them. He scurried after them, elated to be included.

The nurse weighed Addie then left them in a sterile exam room. When the doctor came in, he addressed Emma and Addie and then extended his hand to Carter. "I hadn't realized you'd remarried."

"That's my Papa C," Addie said proudly, which made the adults chuckle.

Addie sat on the paper-covered table and the doctor examined her joints while carrying on a conversation with both Addie and Emma about how she'd been feeling these past few months.

"Any side effects to the biologics medicine?" he questioned.

"No," Emma stated. "It's been a godsend."

"I get that from about twenty percent of my patients. I'm glad it is also working for Addie." He patted her knee and Emma lifted her back into her lap while the doctor settled in his rolling chair.

"Have you been tired a lot, Addie?" he asked.

Addie pushed her head deeper into her mother's chest. "She does seem more tired than her siblings at the end of the day. And seems to need a break or two during the day, especially when they're actively playing and running. But overall, she's barely having the stiffness problem that brought us to see you."

"Good. I'm glad. I'm hoping that, over time, the fatigue and minor joint pain will completely go away. At that time we can discuss weening her off the biologics medicine, but I'm getting ahead of myself." He stood, shook their hands and told Emma to contact the office immediately if Addie started experiencing any new or exaggerated joint pain.

After the doctor left, the three of them moved to the checkout window and Carter took a sleepy Addie in his arms. He didn't care that his hands cramped, Emma needed help and Addie, well, all the triplets, were so adorable and loving that he'd do anything for them.

Emma opened the glass door to leave and led the way to the elevator, pressing the down button and then his elbow. "Thank you. I don't know what I would have done if you hadn't proposed this marriage bargain. The debt I would have gotten myself into…" A flash of worry crossed over her face and then she nibbled on her lower lip, making Carter wonder how she had paid for the first few prescriptions before they were on his plan. But Emma had been clear that wasn't his concern.

Anyway, she had life insurance. Maybe she had dipped into that. Hopefully, she hadn't gotten herself into any debt that she couldn't crawl out of. As an accountant, he liked his clients to pay off their credit cards every month. When he'd reconnected with Robbie six years ago, they'd discussed finances frequently, so he knew Emma and Robbie had never had credit card debt, which was the worst kind of debt to have.

The elevator dinged and the doors opened. At least six people were filling the car. Before Carter could recommend waiting for the next one, Emma stepped on and held the door for him. He entered and shifted Addie so they'd fit around all the people.

"What was I thinking?" Emma said. "With your arthritis, holding Addie must be painful."

She must have seen the twitch of pain cover his face, but did she have to point out his failures to the world? He felt heat rise up his neck as disappointment fisted in his chest.

An older lady shot him a pity look and his stomach dropped that Emma's words were loud enough for all to hear.

When she reached for the little girl, Emma must have noticed his distress at what she'd said because she mouthed, *I'm sorry*. The solemn look on her face spoke to her regret and soothed his pride a bit, but the words hurt just the same.

She took Addie from him, leaving Carter to stand there with empty arms feeling like a spotlight was shining on him. He gulped. Having a gorgeous woman and an elevator full of strangers notice his biggest failure bruised his ego. He focused on the red letters above the elevator doors, slowly counting down.

Back when they'd just married, he hadn't minded if Emma saw him as a broken man with chronic arthritis. At that time, he'd been Robbie's best friend, just trying to help. But now, for some reason, he wanted her to view him as a whole man.

And for the life of him, he wasn't sure what had changed.

Chapter Eight

The next day, Emma was petting Prancer and murmuring comforting words to him while he leaned against her as though he loved her. He probably did. She sure loved him.

Doc Earl pulled into her drive and proceeded toward her home. Yes! She'd been praying he'd come sooner rather than later. And since Esther was watching the triplets in the playroom, Emma could shadow Doc Earl and ask all the questions that had been floating around in her head.

She gave the buck one last pat. Then she slipped out of the pen and jiggled the gate to ensure it was locked so inquisitive Prancer wouldn't escape. Carter's brothers had come over at the crack of dawn to extend the height of this little isolation pen so that frisky Prancer wouldn't be able to jump out.

Bear and Roxy raced to the drive, staying back from the truck as it slowed to a stop, barking their excitement for a visitor.

She hurried over to Doc Earl's dirty white truck that had a silver box built into the chassis for when he made house calls, and greeted him with a side hug. "Thanks for coming."

"Anytime, dear. I know when I get a text from you, you've tried every option." He smiled at her and then began gathering the items he would need to examine Prancer.

She should have known the veterinarian would come as soon as he could.

Out of the corner of her eye, she spotted Carter stepping down from the RV, as though each step was more painful than the last. She averted her gaze, knowing he didn't want her, or anyone, to pity him. She felt bad she had made his arthritis into a big deal yesterday in the elevator. She hadn't been thinking. As soon as they'd gotten to the car, she'd apologized, but she could tell she had hurt him and she felt horrible about it.

He neared, nodded at the vet, gave a quick pat to each dog and then stepped beside her, close enough that their arms brushed. He nudged the brim of his Stetson, tilting it up ever so slightly as his steadfast eyes met hers. She sank into the assurance that they were in this thing together, hoping he could put the elevator incident in the past.

She appreciated his friendship, but she fretted she was relying too heavily on him.

It was one thing to accept his medical insurance. She'd had no other choice. And to have him step in as father for the triplets made sense because they needed a solid male figure and the children enjoyed having him around. It even made sense to have him live in the RV because the coyote scare had been real. The dogs, even though not fully trained, seemed to be keeping the roaming coyote at bay. But was she leaning on him too heavily, emotionally? Maybe so.

Doc Earl stopped at the small pen and turned. "I can see from here it looks about the same as the picture you sent me yesterday. I'm glad you separated Prancer from the herd. That was the right first thing."

"Same size, same feel. Nothing has changed."

He asked her about any other symptoms, or lack of appetite or energy, but there were none to report.

The three of them entered the pen, securing the gate behind them. She stepped away from Carter as they waited for Doc Earl to examine the buck.

When the exam was over, the vet turned to face them and Carter moved closer so he could hear. His fresh scent tickled her senses, drawing him to her. "You might think it'd be logical to lance this and send the results to pathology, but it could be CL," he said, his features serious. Emma shuddered. Caseous lymphadenitis could be devastating and was the first thing she'd thought when she had seen the lump. "If I lance this and it is CL, then you could lose your whole herd."

She appreciated his caution because she had a friend in a similar situation. When the vet had lanced the abscess, some of the fluid had touched the ground and they hadn't cleaned it up properly. The entire herd had been contaminated. Her friend had lost every goat she'd had. Emma gulped back the fear in her throat.

"My plan is to test and treat for less serious illnesses before moving on to the more challenging situations."

Carter's arm brushed hers while the vet set to work. She found comfort with Carter there.

After Doc Earl applied an iodine treatment, the three of them left the pen, secured the gate behind them and then headed to the vet's truck.

"Text me in a few days to give me an update. Especially if it hasn't gotten any smaller." She heard the concern in the vet's voice. She had thought Doc Earl, the professional, would look at the lump and know exactly how to treat it, but he'd been as flummoxed as she.

As the vet drove away, she groaned her frustration. "What if Prancer doesn't make it?" Doc Earl's truck became blurry with the tears in her eyes. Her heart squeezed at the thought of losing Robbie's buck.

Carter bumped her shoulder with his. "With Doc Earl on the job?" He chuckled. "The buck will be just fine."

What if he wasn't? The worry eating her up made her almost lean forward and hug Carter. But she didn't because they were just friends. And just friends didn't hug. Instead, she took a step back, putting a little distance between them.

"I've just started gaining momentum

with selling registered babies. I mean this past spring I sold eighteen." And if she sold somewhere in the twenties next spring, she'd be able to pay off a huge chunk of that credit card debt. Maybe even all of it now that she'd applied for the balance transfer from one card to another with the amazing deal of no interest for a year.

"It'll work out." Admiration shined in his eyes and she basked in it.

The sound of little feet stampeding down the two steps at the back door and squeals of excitement fluttered over. Esther must be getting ready to head out. Emma pasted on a smile for her little ones, pushed a lock of errant hair away from her face and smoothed her shirt before she took a step into the backyard to greet the children and thank Esther for watching them so faithfully.

She crouched low to accept hugs from her littles. Robbie's sweet children.

And prayed the iodine treatment would

fix Prancer's lump. Because that buck was her ticket to getting out of debt.

"It's been almost a week and we still don't know what's wrong with Prancer," Emma stated, frustration lacing her tone as they pushed the girls in the swings while the clouds rolled in. She had caught her bottom lip with her teeth, a sure sign of how anxious she felt about the buck.

The buck's condition hadn't changed between when Doc Earl had come out four days ago and today. Carter had hoped this second visit would fix things, but apparently not. His heart broke for his wife as he gently pushed Cassie on her swing.

"I'm sorry I missed Doc Earl's visit this morning. What happened?" He'd been pulled into a last-minute meeting and caught glimpses of the visit through the blurry window of the RV.

Emma sighed and brushed a piece of hay from her shirt. She wore the minute traces of dirt, goat hair and the faint odor of what she'd coined "unique goaty smell" well. "He did throat and windpipe testing and gave me an anti-inflammatory medication to administer to Prancer. Now we wait."

Carter frowned. He had hoped the visit today would be more conclusive.

A warm breeze stirred strands of her hair that had escaped from her ponytail. A few wispy pieces clung to her long, dark lashes and he itched to brush them away. Instead, he jammed a hand in his pocket.

He racked his brain to come up with a solution. The obvious answer was to purchase another buck. But he wouldn't make the mistake of offering to purchase it for her. Money was clearly a trigger for her.

"I know you don't want me to purchase a buck for you, but you made nice money in the spring selling the baby goats. You could purchase one."

What looked like guilt crossed over her face, but she turned away before he could figure out what she was thinking. Was she hiding something from him? The overdue bill came to mind. Was she in financial trouble? No, if there was anything serious, she'd tell him.

"Carter, it would take a lot of time and research to find a buck of the proper caliber. You know my stock is registered and papered. I'm sticking with Prancer." She lifted her chin but something lingering in her eyes didn't sit well and he wondered if she was keeping something from him. "Besides, I'm planning to purchase another in the spring when I can snag a baby buck. A buckling is cheaper than full-grown and, as you know, springtime is baby time. I'll be inside fixing lunch," she stated and then turned and walked into the house.

"Look at me," Mikey said from the ornamental crepe myrtle tree.

Carter nodded at his enthusiasm then gave both girls a gentle push while they tried to pump and get some momentum going on the swing. He tilted his neck for a little stretch. Thirty minutes and he had another meeting.

He hadn't expected the triplets and goat farm to be so exhausting. On the other hand, he hadn't expected this great joy from being part of a family unit, part of a farm business and a partner in marriage. His heart thudded at his new and rewarding life.

Emma's head bobbed in the little kitchen window as she prepared lunch. He turned to look at Mikey, but he wasn't in the little crepe myrtle anymore. Adrenaline shot through his system. Where had Mikey gone?

Then Carter spotted him in the huge oak tree beside the ornamental myrtle. He must have climbed to the top of the ornamental and somehow gotten on an oak limb. Carter's heartbeat surged at the height the little boy was at. He opened his mouth to tell him to come down when he heard the limb crack. He started for the tree, but the limb and Mikey fell suddenly.

A fearful scream followed by a sickening thud.

Carter raced the few more steps to see Mikey roll over, clutching his arm. His face was contorted in pain.

Before Carter could say or do anything, Emma rushed over to comfort her son.

"It hurts, Mommy," Mikey said, tears streaming down his face.

"I know, baby," she told him. Then, under her breath, she asked Carter to get her purse and keys and meet her at the truck. And could he stay and keep an eye on the girls for her?

He was in shock that Emma could think so clearly in the midst of a crisis, but Carter jumped up and ran into the house. He sent his mother a quick text about what had happened, asking if she could come down.

He settled Emma's purse in the passenger seat of her extended-cab pickup truck and inserted the key into the ignition. Emma rounded the corner of the house, her three-year-old son gently wedged in her arms, worry clinging to her features.

The way Mikey was hanging on to Emma, Carter wouldn't be a help at this moment, so he opened the back door and moved the car seat restraints away so she'd be able to set him in as easily as possible. Then Carter lifted a prayer to God for Mikey's health and to take the boy's pain and give it to Carter instead.

He stepped back so she could buckle him as Mikey wailed and Emma softly cried. Carter felt so helpless.

"Watch the girls?" she asked as she shut Mikey's door while the boy screamed for her to not leave and rounded the truck.

"Absolutely." The anguish on her face about undid him.

As she opened the truck door, his mother turned into the driveway and his hope soared.

He grabbed the door before she slammed it. "Let me drive," he said.

Her gaze swung from his mother's SUV

to him and back again, relief covering her face.

"You are the best," she said as she climbed into the back seat to be right next to Mikey for the trip.

He waved to his mother, jumped into the driver's seat and drove to the emergency room, praying for Mikey's health and the doctor's wisdom all the way.

Emma's soft words seemed to calm Mikey down on the ride.

How had the boy gotten into the larger tree without Carter noticing? He had to be more vigilant when he was in charge of the triplets.

He stopped at the emergency room doors and dashed around the truck to help Emma and Mikey out. Once they slipped through the automatic doors, he parked and hurried to join them.

As he stepped into the brightly lit space, the potent smell of antiseptic cleaner hit him.

Very few people were sitting around the

waiting area. His gaze locked on Emma, who stood under the big registration sign hanging from the ceiling. She was holding Mikey in her arms and peeking over her shoulder, as though looking for Carter. He rushed over to her as she said, "Yes, that's my husband."

Any other day that endearment would make his pulse race, but today Carter's only concern was Mikey.

The sound of rubber soles squeaking against tiled floors filled the air as they followed the nurse to a large room with tall curtains separating the beds. The nurse instructed Emma to lay Mikey on the bed. She gently laid him down, but he refused to let go of her neck with his good arm, so she knelt next to the bed and continued to comfort him with her soothing-mother voice. Soon, the boy seemed relaxed and he let go of Emma's neck. She extracted herself and settled in the one guest chair in the space, keeping her hand on Mikey's unhurt arm for reassurance. Though, Carter wasn't sure if she was trying to reassure Mikey or herself. Before long, Mikey's eyelids closed.

Carter took up position behind Emma, close enough to place his hands on her shoulders. Except, he didn't. "I should have watched him more closely. I'm sorry," he whispered.

She shook her head, though her eyes never left her son. "He's been climbing from the myrtle to the oak all week. I've told him over and over not to, but he persisted." She brushed Mikey's scraggly hair away from his face. "It wasn't your fault, but I bet he learned his lesson today."

The tension Carter had been holding in released because she wasn't blaming him. Her response made Carter care even more for his wife. Whoa. Was he attracted to Emma? If so, this would be the first time since Madison that he'd had feelings for a woman. Something he'd thought would never happen again.

Emma turned and gave him a crooked

grin before returning her attention to Mikey. Her affectionate look wormed its way into Carter's heart. He couldn't help but be drawn to her, but the moment Madison broke up with him flashed through his mind. That instance had formed him into the man he was today. Someone who could never measure up to what Emma deserved.

Beeps surrounded them, along with squeaky shoes and people rushing.

He gazed down at Emma and Mikey. Could he be living in fear?

The realization hit him like a jolt.

If so, he'd done the safest thing possible and married someone who could never fall in love with him.

What a dork. But the twist was that something seemed to be brewing between them, even though neither of them intended on having a real relationship.

He studied his wife as she soothed Mikey. Her long blond ponytail trailed over her shoulder. Wisps of her hair had escaped free and laid on her sun-darkened shoulders. Was it even prudent to consider feelings for someone who was still mourning the death of her husband?

Robbie. He scuffed a hand over his face. He shouldn't be attracted to his best friend's wife. He really shouldn't.

The last thing he wanted was to betray Robbie.

What did it matter? God had brought them together to be a team, to help each other. He should be grateful for the opportunity. Not long for more.

The nurse and orderly rolled Mikey's gurney away so his arm could get x-rayed, leaving her alone with Carter.

"What if his arm is broken?" Emma asked, her hands fisted against her lips.

"Then we'll deal with it," Carter responded, running his fingers through his thick hair. He was worried and that made Emma feel like she wasn't in this emergency alone. "At least he didn't bump his head or anything like that."

She pressed her eyes closed as the room spun at the thought. Beeps from another patient kept going off at irregular intervals. She hadn't even thought about a head injury. She thanked God that his only injury appeared to be his arm. She wanted to turn to Carter and tip her head into his strong chest. Have his comforting arms circle her. Instead, she used her Lamaze technique from childbirth to try to catch her breath for the first time since seeing Mikey fall out of the oak tree and being helpless to stop him.

How had Carter gotten his mother to come to the house so quickly? Emma's knees had felt weak at the thought of driving Mikey here all by herself. Because of Carter's quick thinking, she'd been able to comfort Mikey from the back seat while her husband had capably driven them here.

She was so grateful for Carter's presence. His caring nature drew Emma to him like bees to honey.

Though he had always loved and cherished the triplets, he also now seemed fully invested in the goat farm and the family store. Her mind traveled to their conversation earlier about Prancer and how Carter had almost tried to fix her problem with money. A smile tugged at her lips. She now knew Carter liked to fix things. And since he had some money in the bank, that was his solution for everything. She was honored that he thought enough of her to offer but she needed to remain independent.

"Hopefully we won't have to stay long," she said.

"I imagine they'll patch Mikey up and send him home pretty fast. I bet we'll be checking out quicker than you think."

She sucked in a breath at the thought of the checkout process. "Carter, thank you."

He cocked his head in question.

"For getting us on your gold-plated insurance. I thought the only benefit would be Addie's monthly medication cost. But this hospital visit on my old insurance would have been mostly out-of-pocket payment."

"My pleasure." He shot her a dashing grin. "I'm enjoying being Papa C."

She gazed up at Carter as he studied his phone. He probably had some emergency at work. Him being here felt so right.

She frowned. Wait. What was happening? She took a step away and found the green-vinyl guest chair in the corner.

If he hadn't been on his phone, she probably would have sunk into his arms and allowed him to comfort her.

She clasped her hands in her lap and squeezed tight to force her emotions not to go haywire.

Did she have more-than-friend feelings for Carter? She hoped not.

She was the mother of three. She didn't have time and energy to devote to whatever might be percolating between them.

Before she could mull over her mounting feelings, the squeaky shoes neared them and Mikey's gurney returned. Her boy was sound asleep with a plaster cast on his arm, extending from his palm to below the elbow. Thankfully it appeared he'd be able to use his fingers.

She stepped next to his bed, Carter following, and laid her hand on Mikey's unhurt arm. His warm skin made her feel more confident that he'd be okay. Other than the cast, he looked perfectly normal. He was still her rough-and-tumble boy. Her heart sighed that he was back with them.

"We gave him a little pain reliever and I guess the excitement of the day combined with the medicine knocked him out," the nurse whispered to her.

The doctor entered the tiny space, focused on an electronic tablet in his hands. "Mr. and Mrs. McCaw?"

Emma startled at the name. She was used to Mrs. Bailey. "Yes," she said, cheeks pinking. She kept her hand on Mikey and focused on the man.

The doctor turned the tablet toward them with an X-ray of something on the screen, likely Mikey's arm. "No break, but he has a fracture on the forearm, so he'll have to wear this cast on his arm for four to six weeks."

Relieved that it was only a fracture and not a break—or worse, a head injury—Emma nodded.

She breathed deeply, inhaling the antiseptic smells hospitals were known for, as the man with the white coat flipped the cover on the tablet and stuck it in his pocket. "Any questions?" He lifted his brows for a moment, giving them his full attention.

Her mind went blank. She was just happy to have Mikey back with her. Thankfully, Carter was smart enough to ask if the cast could get wet. How to treat Mikey's pain. If her boy could bathe. When was the next follow-up appointment? The questions she would have thought of on the quiet drive home. One more reason she was grateful he was with her today.

The doctor answered all of Carter's well-thought-out questions. Her husband's strength made her feel cherished and cared for. She appreciated him being with her during this crisis. Maybe too much.

She had her little pack comprising herself and the triplets, and she was unsure about letting Carter in any more than she had because she didn't want anyone, especially the triplets, to think she was replacing their daddy.

This marriage of convenience was supposed to be more like a business transaction.

How had feelings come into play?

She wasn't sure, but she needed to stop this foolishness and get back to the reason they'd married. Insurance. That was it.

Chapter Nine

"Is that all, Mrs. Weaver?" Emma placed the glass jar of goat milk on the counter while Carter waited by the jams and relishes. If they had left the house five minutes earlier, they wouldn't have been delayed by the arrival of her family store customer. Carter immediately felt bad for that thought because he would rather Emma have this sale than spend an extra ten minutes with her at the coffee shop.

"Can I have three jars of those yummy bread and butter pickles? Oh, and Esther Woodward told me about your strawberry jalapeño jam. Just one of those, if you have it?"

Carter efficiently pulled the items from the rustic shelving unit and handed them to Emma.

Her fingers brushed his and a tingle scurried up his arm. He hadn't expected her nearness to affect him this way. He attempted to keep his face neutral so that Mrs. Weaver wouldn't notice.

Emma placed the jars into a four-pack paperboard carrier with a handle. "Anything else?"

"I think that's it for today." Mrs. Weaver turned to Carter. "You two work well as a team." And then she winked.

Carter held the door open for her as she walked out with her purchases.

"Let me get your door for you." Carter rushed past her and opened their customer's car door.

Mrs. Weaver placed her goodies in the empty passenger seat, waved and drove off.

"I'm so glad we were still here to help her," Emma said as she settled in his sedan.

Carter pulled out of their driveway and steered the car toward downtown Serenity. He snuck a glance at Emma. The sparkle in her eyes and the smile that teased her lips suggested she was excited about their little outing. Good. His shoulders relaxed. He had been concerned her mind would be on the triplets back home, in his mother's care. Four long days had passed since Mikey had fallen out of the tree and they'd taken him to the hospital. She'd been overprotective of her little ones since, and he didn't blame her.

Less than ten minutes later, he parked in an angled spot in downtown Serenity and they both exited the sedan, him with a binder in his left hand.

"It's so weird to not have my littles with me. I can't think of the last time," she said, then paused and her face pinked. "The day we got married was probably the last time," she murmured as he opened the door to Morning Grind.

He grinned that their wedding day made her flush. In the moment, the ceremony hadn't felt special, more like procedural. But as time had passed, he reminisced about that day with increasing fondness.

The earthy smell of coffee wafted by as they both studied the chalkboard for a moment before she stepped up and ordered her favorite coffee drink and a seven-layer bar. Yum. He decided on a black coffee with milk, no sugar-filled dessert. Once Emma had found research to suggest that the antioxidants from coffee combined with the protein from cow's milk were encouraged on an anti-inflammatory diet, he'd been able to switch from bitter black coffee to a creamy beverage.

After he paid, he placed his hand on her back and led her to a cozy bistro table in the back. She settled in a chair, placing the plate with the seven-layer bar on the table. He set the leather binder in front of him, excited beyond measure to see her reaction to his news.

"Want some?" She raised her brows and tilted the plate. The sugary essence wafted over.

He raised a palm. "No thanks." He didn't know *what* was making his arthritis feel better, but he would not risk it for a sugary treat.

"This is so nice," she said as she leaned back in her cushioned armchair. "I don't get moments of peace and quiet very often anymore." Maybe not, but even in her harried moments, she was a ray of sunshine. Spending time with Emma was something Carter had been enjoying more with each passing day.

When Emma tossed him a charming smile, his pulse sped up. Whether or not he liked it, his interest in her was growing.

The barista came over with their drinks in big, fat mugs like they'd had in that sitcom from the nineties. Steam rose from their beverages. The coffee and milk mixed into an almost sweet aroma that made his stomach growl. "Enjoy," she said and then rushed back to the counter to serve the people who had just arrived. Both coffees had a white heart formed with the milk foam. His cheeks heated as he remembered the entire town assumed they'd married because they were in love.

He lifted his bright red mug to Emma. She followed suit. "To the family store," he said and then gently tapped his mug to hers in a celebratory toast.

After he took a sip, he rounded the table, slid the ledger in front of her and leaned down so he could see her reaction. "With the cakes and pies from the baker in Love Valley and your new desserts, you have *surpassed* the number you've been hoping for." Since he'd originally told her that she'd met her goal, he enjoyed the surprised look that she had actually exceeded her target. He then named the amount.

She squealed, jumped up and threw her arms around his neck.

She smelled like flowers and summer all rolled into one. He tightened his arms around her and closed his eyes. He shouldn't enjoy this so much, but holding Emma was exhilarating.

It felt so good, but, just as quickly as she'd reached for him, she jumped back and mumbled an apology. That she had gotten carried away.

He almost nodded because he got it. Even though he was more aware of Emma lately than he liked, his past heartbreak made him wary. He couldn't take that risk a second time.

She settled back in her seat. "I mean I knew that I had reached my goal. But surpassed it by that much? Wow."

For reasons he didn't understand, meeting this goal had been important to her, so he was thrilled for her. Hoping she'd be able to recreate her success, he tapped the line of tidy numbers.

"See here," he said. Then he explained the financial difference between this month and last. "Even after this big withdrawal, you've brought your bottom line into the black." Though he was curious, he would not ask her about the withdrawal. That was her business.

She gulped and something like worry crossed over her face. Maybe he shouldn't have mentioned the big withdrawal. Now he had to assure her that what was on the spreadsheet was good news.

He crouched down so they could be at eye level. And so other patrons could not overhear. "I thought you'd want to know the details so you could replicate the success."

"Carter, I have dyscalculia. Numbers don't make any sense to me," she whispered.

He pulled his head back in surprise and, just like that, the withdrawal and what it was for became unimportant. The flash of pain in her pretty eyes landing with the force of a physical blow. He'd tutored someone in college who'd struggled with processing math-related concepts. Cases could be mild to severe and many people with the ailment were highly intelligent. That explained why Robbie had reached out to him years before to handle the family store books.

"I'm sorry. That must be so hard." His chest ached that she had to walk through life with this math disability.

"I've survived."

"Oh, Emma, you more than survived."

She shrugged as though it was no big deal, but it was. He wanted to ask so many questions but closed his mouth and shoved the paperwork into his binder.

As he settled in his seat, a light bulb clicked and he realized why she had customers pay with an app or check instead of cash. Cash would make her have to count out the change. In fact, she used financial software to enter her deposits and withdrawals automatically, probably because of her learning disorder.

What he had hoped would be a time of

celebration had turned into what appeared to be a humiliating moment for Emma.

His phone buzzed with an incoming email. He pulled it out and scanned the message from her accounting software that notified him of changes. His heart raced at the notification.

"Emma, I think there's some type of fraud happening on your business credit card. There's been a large balance transferred from some other account to yours." He turned his phone so she could read the email herself. "You need to call your credit card company right away." The words flew out of his mouth so quickly, they ended up in a blur.

She glanced at his phone and then leaned back in her chair. Her eyebrows were scrunched together and she rolled in her bottom lip as though concerned, and she should be! This was obvious identity theft. She had frozen her credit with the credit agency to protect herself, right? He sure hoped so. But then, why was she sitting there not moving?

"Carter, that was me. I transferred the balance from another card to my business card about a week ago. I'm not sure why it took that long to post." She studied the wooden tabletop. Clearly, she hadn't considered that he would receive a notification when the balance transfer took effect. "I had a large balance from the first few biologics prescription purchases that I couldn't pay off. This card offered me a deal I couldn't refuse. Transfer the balance and forgo paying interest for twelve months." Her chin was set in that *I can handle it* position.

He felt his mouth open in shock. She had a large credit card balance she couldn't pay and she hadn't told him?

He had funds in the bank. He could pay some of the debt for her. But as he opened his mouth to say so, her features tightened.

"I can handle this, Carter." Her tone wavered with emotion and two worried commas appeared above her brows. "I have a plan to pay it off when I sell the spring babies." When her chin lifted, he remembered her strong desire for independence.

He wished she would accept his financial help, but he had to respect her decision.

The next morning, Emma waited in the kitchen for the coffee to brew, inhaling the bitter aroma that, as a teen, she used to hate but now could not get through the day without. She turned over the events of the prior day. She could not believe she hadn't remembered that Carter had access to her books and would see the balance transfer the moment it came across. Thankfully, he'd allowed her to drop the topic. Though her financial situation was hers to deal with, she was warming to how concerned he was about her life and how he longed to resolve all her problems. At first, his desire to fix things had made her feel vulnerable. But she now understood he was only trying to help. Over this past month, appreciation for her sweet husband grew with each passing day.

"Morning," Carter said as he stepped into the kitchen that glowed with the sunrise. He gave her a wide grin that made her insides tumble.

She simply smiled back, afraid to speak since she might bring up that spontaneous hug from yesterday and embarrass herself yet again. His gaze dropped to his phone as heat rose in her cheeks at the mere thought of the moment in the coffee shop. She turned to the machine and focused on the dripping coffee so he wouldn't see her embarrassment. He had probably thought she was being forward with that excited hug she had given him. Though he was her husband and they were friends, she didn't have the right to hug him whenever she wanted.

She wasn't sure what affected her most—his good looks or her surprising attraction to him. Seemed no matter how hard she tried to suppress it, her awareness of him kept building.

And since he was too fearful of another relationship, she knew her growing feelings would never be reciprocated. Which was fine with her.

He had planned to remain a bachelor until the rapture, but then she'd needed medical insurance, so he'd helped a friend. There was no romance brewing on his end. She knew that.

The drip finally stopped. She filled her travel mug and then moved over to the refrigerator to add a little milk. One, because she wanted to get out of his way. Two, because lately his nearness made her pulse race.

"So, Doc Earl is coming out today?" Carter asked while he fixed his coffee and they readied themselves to get as many chores done as possible before the triplets woke up. Like every morning.

"No, tomorrow."

They moved to the side door to slide

on their muck boots. Through this whole Prancer lump thing, Carter had been a champ. She'd needed to focus on Prancer twice a day for a variety of medicines that Doc Earl thought would resolve the lump. None of them had. But regardless, getting medicine into a goat wasn't easy and that meant Carter had been on daddy duty more since she'd discovered the buck's lump. He had been emotionally reassuring and understanding during this time, which she found comforting.

They walked out to the goat pen, reviewing what they were planning to do and in what order.

"Where's Roxy?" she asked, craning her neck to see beyond the little structure toward the back of the spacious pen, looking for the Great Pyrenees who lived in the pen with the female goats. Bear was in the boy's pen, but he appeared agitated as he paced back and forth against the fence line closest to the girl's pen.

"I don't see her," Carter said, worry

laced his tone as he looked around. The coffee Emma had just consumed soured in her stomach.

She opened the pen and rushed around, searching every spot the dog may have hidden, but Emma knew Roxy didn't hide. She always acted like she was on duty. The dog seemed to sleep with one eye open, so where was she?

Emma sucked in a breath. "Dolly's gone, too!"

"Look at this." Carter crouched low and pointed to a section of fence that appeared to be lifted.

"Could Dolly have fit through there?"

"I don't think so, but let me look at the cameras to see what happened."

Emma scanned the adjacent property and didn't see the dog or goat. Had the coyote been back? Maybe the coyote had been successful and guard dogs weren't the answer.

Her heart raced. What had happened to the dog and goat?

"Yup," Carter said as he stared at his phone. "Dolly lifted the fencing with her horns and slipped through while Roxy was nipping at her to stop. Once Dolly got through, the Great Pyrenees paced back and forth and then lunged over the fence. It looks like she followed Dolly, maybe to guard her?"

Emma sucked in a worried breath then took the phone and watched the video at double speed to see for herself. "What are we going to do?" she asked as she handed the device back to Carter. She could barely catch her breath at the missing goat and dog. Things couldn't get much worse.

"I'll have Autumn come over. She might know what to do." He took charge. "You text or call all your neighbors to be on the lookout. Who knows, maybe someone has seen the pair?"

"On it," she said, focusing on her phone.

As soon as she finished sending her last neighbor a text, Addie started calling to her over the monitor.

Emma went into the house to get the triplets and set up breakfast. Adrenaline shot through her system. How could she carry on like normal when everything was far from normal? But her babies needed her, even if there were missing animals to find.

Carter stepped into the house, kicked off his muck boots and washed his hands. "I did a quick fix on the fence so no one else can get out that same way."

She hadn't even thought of other goats escaping in the same manner. Handsome and handy? She couldn't help but take notice of how he'd taken charge when she'd been at a loss. *Thank You, Lord, for providing me with Carter.*

The hum of a vehicle pulling into the driveway sounded. Must be Autumn.

Carter's sister stepped through the side door, not bothering to take off her shoes. A serious expression covered her face. "I'm going to drive around." Her words were quick and clipped. "I sent a text to everyone I know in the area. They are keeping an eye out and if they have cameras, they will watch the feed to see if they can offer any clues."

"I want to go with you," Emma stated as she cracked another egg into the mixing bowl.

"We can load the triplets into the minivan," Carter said as he hefted Mikey onto his hip.

"No," Emma stated. She wiped her hands on the dishtowel and then touched his shoulder. "Can you finish feeding them? I'll go with Autumn to look. Anyway, I want you here in case Roxy and Dolly return." Her voice hitched at the last part. *Please, God, keep them both safe.*

He put a squirming Mikey on the floor while he aimed a caring look at her. "Of course, go. Find them!"

She gave him a quick hug but stepped back swiftly. Why did she keep doing that? Except, this time, it had felt right.

His hands had slipped around her waist like they belonged.

She shook off the notion, grabbed her purse and followed Autumn out to her beat-up minivan.

"What was that?" Autumn asked as she took off toward the mailbox.

"What?"

"You like my brother."

"Do not."

"Emma, we're not in grade school. You do, too. It's so obvious."

She turned her face toward the open window as her cheeks heated, searching the landscape for the Great Pyrenees and the missing goat. "Maybe I'm starting to have feelings for him, but Robbie was my one true love."

Silence enveloped the van as Autumn crawled along the barely traveled road searching for the missing animals.

"So you're saying," Autumn asked softly, "you are afraid to fall for my little brother because you don't want to taint Robbie's memory?"

"Yes," she said. "I mean no. I mean... I guess so."

"Sweetie, you remember that Robbie encouraged you to remarry one day, right?" Autumn said in a gentle tone.

With her arm resting on the open car window, a rush of breeze blew a lock of hair from Emma's face. She pulled those deep conversations she and Robbie had shared from the depths of her memory. When they'd known he'd be gone soon, he had talked with her about her future. He had wanted to guide her in her choices for the years ahead. Give her advice and the freedom to move on. Her throat tightened.

"Remember how he said he wanted you to have a life partner, not just because he wanted the triplets to have a dad to grow up with, but told you to keep your heart open to another love?"

Emma's heart hiccupped at the vivid memory. Yes. Autumn had been watching the triplets that day. After Robbie had had his say, he'd fallen asleep and she'd taken comfort in her good friend's arms. Weeping as she'd told Autumn all that Robbie had said. Not wanting to believe she'd lose him soon and become a widow. That day was the moment his imminent death had felt all too real.

Somehow, with Robbie's illness and death, Emma had blocked those conversations out. Robbie had wanted her to be open to falling in love again.

After they had searched for miles, Autumn dropped Emma at her front porch without Roxy and Dolly, stating she and her family would continue to pray for the safety of the animals and that they'd be found safe soon.

But what if they weren't?

Autumn drove away while Emma took in the goat farm she had built with Robbie. This place and the triplets were her priorities. Yet, in the past month, her only buck had a mysterious lump that might ruin her plans to sell baby goats in the spring, she'd lost one of her guard dogs and a precious doe, and the debt she'd gotten herself into seemed less manageable with each passing day.

Tears threatened but she pushed them away and held her head high. Somehow, she needed to rein in the chaos that had become her life.

Chapter Ten

The feel of Carter's arms tightening around her waist yesterday morning flooded Emma's senses and made her wonder. She shook off the memory, stepped out the kitchen door into the bright sunshine and breathed deeply, willing her pounding headache to go away. All three children had woken cranky, and the day hadn't gotten any better. They'd probably been thrown off by the upsetting disappearance of Roxy and Dolly. So, midmorning, Emma had put them down for a nap, thinking they'd needed a little quiet time and, shockingly, they had all fallen fast asleep.

The sun felt nice warming her face, but she had better get moving. She strode over to the goat pen and scanned the area, as though the dog and goat would have miraculously returned while she'd been in the house. But neither was there. She checked her phone. No missed calls or text messages about a possible sighting. She released a worried sigh.

At least she wouldn't have three children to corral when Doc Earl arrived to check on Prancer, assuming the triplets remained asleep. Too anxious over the missing dog and goat, Emma flipped a bucket upside down, took a seat beside the goat pen gate and did the only thing she could think of that might help: she began praying for the safe return of Roxy and Dolly.

Except, what Autumn had said to her yesterday afternoon in the dog-hair-covered minivan kept interrupting her prayer. Her friend's reminder that Robbie had wanted her to remarry had jolted her. But now, after spending some time with the notion, she was finally accepting that Robbie was gone, and she had to let him go. Even if she moved on, she could still keep Robbie's memory alive. Carter would help because he was a thoughtful and sympathetic friend.

Which brought her right back to that quick hug yesterday. She was sure Carter's arms had tightened around her waist. Had he done that because he was concerned about the missing animals or because he cared for her?

The sound of a vehicle approaching interrupted her thoughts and she whipped her head around, hoping for good news about the missing dog and goat. But it was only Doc Earl. Her disappointment quickly turned to hope when she remembered what he was there for. Prancer.

She stowed the bucket and hurried to greet the veterinarian as Carter opened the RV door and made his way over.

"I heard about Roxy and Dolly," Doc Earl said, compassion lacing his tone. "Everyone is searching. They'll turn up. I'm sure they will." He patted her shoulder. "Roxy is smart. She's probably somewhere fiercely guarding Dolly."

Tears pricked the backs of her eyes. He was right, the dog and goat would turn up. They had to.

After a quick examination of Prancer's lump, Doc Earl announced there was no change. "I've been thinking about this buck since I was here last," the veterinarian said. "I think it's time to lance the lump to see what we're dealing with."

She nodded, then swallowed down the panic crawling up the back of her throat. They discussed the procedure and her fear over Prancer's long-term health ratcheted up. Carter's presence calmed her. She wanted to reach for his hand but settled on releasing a nervous breath instead.

Doc Earl went to his truck to get the supplies while she looked into Carter's steadfast eyes. As their gazes met, her stomach flip-flopped with interest. She shook off the emotion. It wasn't attraction, she told herself. It was gratitude that he cared about the herd as much as she did.

"It'll be okay," Carter said in a soft and reassuring voice. He closed his hand around hers and their fingers interlaced, sending a thrill up her arm. "We need to trust in Doc Earl. And at this point, we don't have any other choices."

She looked into Carter's confident face and knew he was right. She breathed a silent prayer that the lancing would go smoothly. The warmth from Carter's hand buoyed her nervous and worried heart. Prancer might only be a goat, but to her he was family.

Once Doc Earl returned to the pen where Prancer had been isolated, he began preparing to lance the wound. Emma squeezed Carter's hand. Maybe it wasn't wise to lean on him, but she couldn't help it. Not when Prancer's health was on the line.

She watched Doc Earl's practiced hands

as he performed the short procedure. "Hmm, this does not appear to be consistent with CL," he stated as he capped the syringe and put it in his bag.

She let out a huge sigh of relief and released Carter's hand to tuck an errant lock of hair behind her ear. Doc Earl's announcement eased her mind because anything other than CL was something she could deal with. Hopefully.

He cleaned the site and proceeded to look into Prancer's mouth. How the veterinarian got the buck to keep his mouth open without slicing the man's fingers, she had no idea. But she was thankful for Prancer's cooperation.

"I think I see the problem," he said as he shined a light into the buck's mouth. Emma moved beside him and craned her neck to see what Doc Earl was looking at. "There is a small wound on the inner throat that has healed with a tiny scar." He took his hands out of Prancer's mouth, gave him a small treat and then pocketed his small flashlight.

"I bet the buck somehow got a cut in his throat and it became infected," he continued. "I'll send this sample to the lab and they can tell us what type of infection we are dealing with."

Doc Earl collected his belongings and packed them in his truck. He told her it would be a couple of days to find out the pathology results and left.

Now that they were pretty sure it wasn't CL, they could fix it. The question was, would Prancer be ready for breeding season? Because if he wasn't, she wouldn't have kids to sell in the spring to pay off the credit card debt.

Sturdy Carter stood a few feet away, watching as Doc Earl's vehicle left gravel dust swirling above the drive.

She yearned to tip her head against Carter's strong and able shoulder, but she didn't. The whole hand-holding thing earlier might have been a mistake, and she didn't want to add to it.

Her childhood as a cast-off orphan had taught her she was safer when she didn't put herself out there. So maybe friendship was the best route with Carter. After all, that's what their original agreement was for.

The triplets had woken shortly after Doc Earl left and Emma was preparing lunch. Carter had offered to help, but she'd declined. The funny look on her face had made him a smidge nervous. Maybe he shouldn't have held her hand earlier when Doc Earl was here. He'd been trying to comfort her, but maybe she'd taken it the wrong way? As Emma placed a bowl off to the side, he roughed a hand over his face.

"Thanks for your help," Emma said and then flashed him a strained smile.

"Happy to," he responded then carried the three small bowls over to the table and placed the grape halves in front of the children, who eagerly gobbled them up. Even though they weren't fully aware of the threat of Roxy and Dolly's disappearance, the children still seemed preoccupied with the situation. Who was he kidding? They all were.

He picked up the bowl of cubed chicken and returned to the children, dropping a small handful in front of each. Though Carter had had back-to-back meetings early this morning, the rest of the day was pretty free. If he had to, he could put some time in after the triplets went to bed tonight. With how worried Emma was with Prancer and her edginess about the pathology results, she seemed like she needed some support right now. Or at least someone to talk through what had just happened with Prancer.

That was why he'd not questioned her about the credit card balance transfer. What had she been thinking? He could afford to help her pay that balance off in a couple of months. She shouldn't wait until baby season and risk having her credit score dip. Somehow, he'd have to approach this topic. But now, while the goat and dog were missing, was not the right time.

Emma eyed the children, all happily eating, then she wiped her hands on a dish cloth and looked out the window. "I miss Roxy and Dolly," she whispered.

He placed his hand on her shoulder to comfort her. The heat at their connection jumbled his thoughts, and the words he'd been about to say flew right out the open window.

"Thank you for figuring out what happened with that inquisitive goat. I hadn't even thought about the video surveillance yesterday morning," she said as she turned and picked up two plates with cheese cubes, small crackers and fresh strawberries from his mother's garden. His hand dropped from her shoulder and gradually his thoughts cleared. She placed the plates in front of the girls while he placed the third plate in front of Mikey, who somehow managed to play and eat with that bulky cast on his arm. "And thanks for fixing the fence that Dolly lifted. I hadn't thought of that, either."

Oh, he got what was bothering her. She was concerned she was leaning on him too heavily. That if he hadn't been around, the rescue efforts wouldn't have taken place. She was so wrong. Other than his mother, she was the strongest woman that he knew.

He gathered the empty grape bowls and stuck them in the dishwasher. "You did great, Emma. Yes, I noticed the fence and thought of the videos before you, but if I weren't here, you'd have come to the same conclusion as I did." She turned to look at him and he could see in her eyes she wasn't sure if she could have handled the situation on her own.

"Thanks," she said and gave him a smile that didn't quite reach her eyes. Then she started washing the cutting board and knife.

He racked his brain for a topic that would lift her spirits. "The good news is that when I had to kneel and fix the fence, my joints felt much better than they have," he said, getting a little excited thinking of the moment again. Amidst the chaos of the missing animals, he hadn't realized until now his lack of pain when he had knelt to do the work. "I really appreciate that you investigated arthritis and recommended the diet change. On the advice of my doctor, I also started collagen and supplements. I'm not sure what's making me feel better, but I feel more like I did at seventeen than a month ago."

A smile lit her face at his encouraging words.

"I'm sorry you felt sore at such a young age," she said.

He shrugged. "I didn't mind that as much as how my girlfriend dumped me like a hot potato right before I proposed because she didn't want to date an invalid." Man, that still hurt.

"Oh, Carter, you are far from an invalid." Her facial reaction wasn't one of pity, more like a shared compassion. Even though he hadn't meant to be so transparent and share Madison's cruel words, his spirits lifted that he had married well. "Just so you know," Emma continued, "your girlfriend was a jerk." She placed her warm palm on his shoulder and leaned in.

Right then, his phone rang. He fumbled for it, wondering if they had been about to hug. They'd hugged in the past, but this moment felt different. His heart raced as he answered without looking at the display.

"Your dog and goat are in the east pasture, bro," Ethan said, sounding a little out of breath.

"Roxy and Dolly are at the Triple C," he told Emma. Her face lit up as she leaned forward, waiting for more details. He clicked the speakerphone button and held the phone between them.

Ethan told them the dog was being hyperprotective of the goat, so he was unable to load them up. He thought it'd be best if Carter and Emma could come over to get them. His mother was on her way to watch the triplets. They thanked Ethan and then Carter hung up. Emma grinned at him.

"Can you hook up the old horse trailer to my truck while I finish feeding the children?" Her eyes were bright with excitement.

He kicked on his muck boots and hooked up the trailer. As he was finishing, his mother arrived and Emma shot out of the house, her purse slung around her shoulder. "You can drive." She hopped in the passenger seat and they took off. He prayed Roxy and Dolly were healthy and didn't have any life-threatening injuries.

"Things are finally coming together. Prancer's probably going to be okay. Roxy seems like she's turning into a great working guard dog, at least in this situation."

"I'm grateful," Carter said as he pointed the extended-cab pickup toward the Triple C.

"Your family is the best, you know?" she said. He held in the wry laughter bubbling up in his chest. His siblings tried to give him advice when he didn't want it. And though his parents were amazing, they also could do the same. But he knew she was comparing her childhood against his, which made him sober.

This past month of marriage, combined with an up-close view into Emma's life, had proven to Carter that he was falling for his best friend's wife. Well, his wife now. But she was still in love with Robbie and that fact stung.

He stole a glance at Emma, her hands clasped tight in her lap and leaning forward with such hope for a safe return of her animals. She was stunning and probably had no idea. He drank her in. She mesmerized him like no one ever had.

He felt at ease around her somehow, as if he didn't have to impress her or be someone he wasn't. But just because he'd begun craving spending time with her didn't mean she felt the same.

Would there ever come a day when she'd see him as more than a friend and confidant?

His mind played their coffee shop celebration a few days ago. That was fun. Perhaps he could date her. His heart stuttered at the thought. Would she be interested in even trying to see if she could have feelings for him?

As he drove the truck onto the Triple C, he let the idea settle. That might work. With this plan in mind, he felt the burden over how she felt toward him release. He slowed as he entered the bumpy pastures. In the distance, he spotted his father's truck, along with Ethan and one of the ranch hands on their horses. In the corner of the pasture, Roxy had cornered Dolly. Relief washed over him at the sight.

Other than some flesh-wound scratches, Dolly seemed fine. And Roxy appeared invigorated by the events of the past couple of days.

Emma loaded Dolly into the trailer and Roxy followed. He was ecstatic they had found the dog and goat unharmed. They thanked his family for their help and headed home.

They returned to her property and exited the truck. As he rounded the horse trailer, Emma caught his hand and his skin tingled at the contact.

"Thank you for everything, Carter. I appreciate how you care as much for our herd as I do."

Our herd. He appreciated she was finally seeing him as a partner.

God had not only provided him a way to be a father, but He'd also given Carter a sweet wife.

Emma made him deliriously happy.

There. He'd said it. But would anything ever come of it? He sure hoped so.

Later that evening, Emma closed the triplets' door and made her way to the kitchen.

Her body ached from a physical day with the goats and chasing after the children. She didn't have the energy to make any desserts for the family store. But she was also wired, so she wasn't ready to turn in yet, either.

"Want to watch a movie?" she asked Carter as they made a quick pass picking up the dinner dishes.

"Only if it isn't a smoochy romance." He winked at her and her tummy somersaulted.

Was he flirting with her? "You can pick." While he closed the dishwasher, she tried to even out her breaths as she finished drying the plastic bowls. This marriage bargain seemed to be turning into something more. At least for her.

"How about a shoot-'em-up action film?"

She shook her head at him, knowing full well he was sweet enough that he'd pick something they'd both enjoy watching.

Her mind recalled what he had said earlier in the day about feeling rejected by his girlfriend because of his diagnosis. Emma steamed that Madison had called him an invalid. He'd been vague with details before but Carter was the furthest thing from an invalid. When he had first shared about his arthritis, right before they'd decided on the marriage of convenience, she'd filed the information in the back of her brain because so much had been happening at the time. She hadn't processed all he'd gone through until today. For the first time, Emma realized that his life was anything but the fairy tale she had always pictured. She'd had no idea that some chapters of his story had been so brutal. Knowing about his past made him seem a bit more human somehow. More relatable.

"Your family has been so helpful with

everything," she said, "especially finding Roxy and Dolly."

"Anyone would do it. No big deal."

"No, Carter, it is a big deal," she retorted. "You probably don't know this, but I actually have family. Except, when I was little, they didn't care enough about me to act like adults, so they ended up losing custody of me." She lifted her chin and refused to get emotional about something that had happened so long ago.

His eyebrows raised but his features gave her the encouragement to continue.

"At seven, after a tumultuous childhood, I ended up in foster care. You know that, but what you don't know is that my mother and father were alive. And I wasn't enough for them." Her voice shook at the unthinkable actions of her parents. "Drugs and alcohol were more important. Did you know I made up a story in foster care?" At his surprised face, she nodded. "To feel like I fit in, I told all the other kids my parents were missionaries and their plane was shot down. I mean what foster child has parents that don't want her?"

Her body had started to shake at the memory. She'd only ever told Robbie those details and she still wasn't sure why she'd blurted it out just now. After a stressful couple of days, all she and Carter wanted was to relax, not listen to her heartbreaking childhood story.

His features were awash with compassion and sorrow, but not pity. Though she wasn't a child anymore, her parents' abandonment shouldn't have such a raw edge to it. But even after all this time, it did.

"That's horrible, Emma. I mean the part about your parents' actions. And I don't blame you. I think I'd make a story like that up, too."

She swallowed the lump in her throat. His kind reaction meant a lot to her. How come she had never made peace with the past? Her parents didn't define her, not by a long shot. Regardless, it felt good getting that secret out in the open. The longer Carter lived in the RV, the more she wanted to open up to him. She stepped over the playroom gate and he followed.

Carter continued. "I know you said your parents used to drop you at church on Sunday mornings before you entered the orphanage."

She gave him a watery smile, remembering her sweet Sunday mornings. "Miss Martha was the best. She shined God's light so strong."

He grinned. "Thank God for Miss Martha. Because of her, when you went to the orphanage, you could rely on God. He was and is your Heavenly Father. You've been grafted into God's family." The moment hung in the air, as though he wanted to say more. But then he winked and focused on his phone as he brought up the movie app and began scrolling.

She settled on the couch and pulled a soft blanket over her legs. The wink caused her tummy to somersault with attraction and also gave her hope. God had been with her when she'd entered the orphanage. He had guided her and comforted her during those years full of trials. Even though her parents had deserted her, God never had. And He never would.

Had she been looking at self-worth wrong all these years?

She shuddered. If she had, then she'd been wrong about many things.

"Found one," he said. He clicked off the lamp beside him and the low television light lit the room.

A comedy that had a little action and a teeny bit of romance came on the screen. One she'd recently added to their list. She turned and smirked at him because he cared enough to pick a movie she'd enjoy.

After the past few days, they needed a few laughs.

"We'll both like this," he said as he settled back on the cushions.

Right now, she wanted to be snuggled beside him, savoring the delightful weight of his arm draped over her shoulder. Instead, she lifted her blanket higher against the chill of the air-conditioning.

His words about being grafted into God's family resonated with her. Healed a wounded part of her heart.

As the opening credits played, he turned his head and studied her. She got caught up with his gaze. Why did the compassion radiating from his eyes make her feel so vulnerable? She gulped as he turned to watch the movie. She was so used to putting up walls because of the wounds she'd carried as an orphan. But she wasn't an orphan anymore. God was her Heavenly Father, and she was an adult with three little children to raise.

She snuck a glance at Carter's profile. He was easy on the eyes, with tanned skin and dark hair that curled up at the bottom like he needed a haircut. Her fingers itched to feel the short stubble lining his jaw, so she clasped them together in her lap. From the other side of the long couch, she could barely smell his masculine scent.

Was she really falling for Carter?

She wasn't sure, but after Autumn reminded her that Robbie hadn't wanted her to pine after him for the rest of her life, she felt like she could move on. Robbie had wanted her to live and perhaps love again.

She liked her husband. He was a good friend. And it felt like maybe their relationship was slowly becoming something more.

And she was okay with that.

Maybe even excited.

But then her mind turned to the hospital bill Carter didn't know about that she'd negotiated into six payments. Since he'd freaked out about the credit card balance transfer, she was hesitant to tell him about the additional debt she'd incurred. She only had four more payments, but still. A month ago, when he'd found the overdue bill, keeping the secret had seemed right, even necessary. Now she wondered if she should say something. Clear the air.

Her insides twisted with indecision.

There was no reason to open that can of worms because the family store was doing well, which meant she was on track to make the final four payments.

She snuggled a little deeper under the cozy blanket as the television screen illuminated the room.

The negotiated bill wasn't really a secret because she was responsible for her own expenses. The payment plan was just another bill.

Anyway, he wasn't ever going to find out about the outstanding payments she was on the hook for, so why was she even worried?

Chapter Eleven

Three days later, Emma was giddy that Prancer's infection had been completely treatable. She dried the last of the lunch dishes while she listened for the triplets to wake from their afternoon nap. The sky was dark and cloudy, but she hoped they could play in the backyard before the skies opened up.

As she put the last of the lunch dishes away, the dogs started barking. She cocked her head at the urgency. That wasn't a warning bark or a playful noise. Something was wrong. She tossed the towel on the counter, stuck her phone in her back pocket and scrambled out the door. Autumn had told her the Great Pyrenees would not bark unless something was wrong. And they wouldn't bark repeatedly. Yet they were both barking loudly and with force.

She reached the corner of the house to see that Bear had jumped the boy pen and was between her and the family store, Robbie's first project on this property. He'd worked so hard to turn that oversized shed into a store for her.

A burning rubber smell hit her as she neared Bear, whose barking became more agitated as he darted from the store and back to her. Her heart raced with the confusing moment.

As she neared the building, the dog darted to the backside of the structure, his barks turning to painful-sounding howls. When she rounded the store, she saw tiny sparks leaping from the refrigeration unit that had been built into the store, with the back of it exposed to the elements. She gasped at the sight.

Even though she knew she should get help, her feet refused to move and her voice wouldn't work. Adrenaline buzzed as stunned helplessness flooded her.

When small flames started to shoot out of the unit, she shook herself out of her dazed state and shouted for Carter. She yanked out her phone, called 9-1-1 and then opened the family store door. The structure looked fine from this angle, but she knew that might not last long. She propped the phone between her shoulder and chin while she told them about the fire emergency and frantically began packing crates with the grass-fed beef from the deep freezer. She had to salvage as much as possible, starting with the most expensive items.

Carter's frame filled the doorway. "I pulled the service breaker next to the unit," he said, huffing from the exertion of racing over. "Nothing changed. The flames are getting taller, but right now it's contained in the refrigeration unit."

"How in the world did it catch fire?"

Carter shrugged. "Malfunction? Loose wire?" He snagged a full crate and rushed it over to the porch while she relayed the updated status to the operator.

She lugged the next crate to her front porch and stacked it on top of the one Carter had brought over. Sprinting back to the store, she noticed Carter unwrapping the hose.

"I'm going to soak the structure to stop the spread of fire," he yelled. Emma prayed the fire would be contained to the refrigeration unit to minimize the loss. "My mother is on her way to watch the triplets if we need her."

God bless the McCaws, and Cora especially. They'd embraced Emma and the triplets as though they were family, which, in a way, they now were.

Hurrying, she reentered the building and set another crate down. There was still a lot of beef in here. The farmer wouldn't be happy if his product burned, so she pushed herself to fill up another load.

"The building has caught fire," Carter declared. "You need to get out of here."

Dread filled her core as she clutched the crate to her chest and picked up the tote bag filled with paperwork from her little desk. She dashed to the front porch and placed them beside the other salvaged items. There was nothing she could do about the items she'd been unable to rescue. She then updated the emergency operator, who said there were units on their way and disconnected the call.

Emma turned. She sucked in a smokey breath as flames curled over the roof. Tears filled her eyes at losing Robbie's very first project.

Carter diligently kept hosing down the structure, hoping to save it.

Please, Lord, don't take my family store away from me. It means too much to me. And to Robbie.

She glanced back to the house, at least sixty yards away. *And please keep our home and children and herd safe as well,* she added to the prayer.

Bear had jumped back into the boys' pen and had herded the two males to the far corner of the pen, as far away from the fire as possible. Roxy had done the same with the females.

The fire was climbing higher up and over the roof, and new flames licked the right and left sides of the structure as well. At the sight, her eyes filled and the building became blurry. She had to do something!

She rushed to their other hose, untangled it and started spraying. The heat from the fire singed her skin. As smoke filled the air, she coughed and tried to cover her mouth. A hazy glow cloaked the area.

She swiped the sweat off her forehead. Defeat closed in as hosing the structure down didn't seem to help.

Her limbs shook at the exertion and fear of what was happening.

She could not lose the family store. The income was integral to her survival and to her paying off the rest of the negotiated hospital bill. Since she didn't have a true job, she paid the bills with her survivor benefits and the income from the store and baby goat sales.

Her unbidden tears began falling and there was nothing she could do to stop them.

Emma's tear-stained face was like a punch in the gut to Carter as they both futilely sprayed water on the burning structure. He coughed at the smoke curling toward him. The flames were tall and engulfed the front of the building. His stomach rolled at the sight of Emma's precious store up in flames.

As the fire blazed, Carter wanted to corral Emma and the triplets into the vehicle and drive them far away from danger, but he knew help was on the way. If nothing else, his mother could take them to the Triple C for safekeeping. Because right now, his only concern were his wife and children. A building could be rebuilt. He didn't even want to entertain losing Emma or one of the triplets.

At the sound of a vehicle approaching, relief washed over Carter like the water he'd been futilely spraying for the past ten minutes. He looked up to see a flood of dusty trucks in the driveway, parking a safe distance away.

His mother, who declared herself on triplet duty, jumped out of the first truck and rushed into the house to see if the children were awake from their nap. Tears welled up behind his eyelids. He could always depend on his family.

His father and brothers and a couple of other ranchers on the street headed over to him with garden hoses. They also had hose splitters so they could connect more hoses to the limited hose bibs on the house.

Everyone acted quickly, but the fire continued to burn, leaving zigzag sections of charred wood. Carter's head was spinning with the suddenness of the blaze. One of his brothers took Emma's hose from her and she crumbled into a heap. He wanted to rush over and take her in his arms, but he had a hose and a job. Autumn went to Emma, settling her arm around his wife.

The air was heavy with the smell of smoke as the front of the structure took off in flames. Three sides of the store were charred and now smoking, leaving just the front engulfed. The building was a total loss, but he prayed the house and children and goats would come out of this unscathed.

Someone seized the hose from him and took over. Not until his hands were empty did his arms start to shake from the exertion of the last fifteen minutes and his hands cramped with arthritic pain.

A fire truck siren wailed in the distance,

but based on what he saw, any additional effort would prove futile.

He shook off the sting from his arms and strode over to Emma, who was now standing and looking toward where the fire truck was coming from. The despair that shimmered in her eyes gutted him.

Autumn cocked her head at him as if to say, *She's your wife, comfort her.* Then his sister headed toward the front porch, probably to help his mother with the triplets and give her a fire report.

He intertwined his fingers with Emma's. In response, she clutched his hand tight. "Oh, Carter, what am I going to do?" She turned and lay her dainty head on his chest, turning her back to the blaze. He circled her with his free arm as she clutched his shirt. The affection felt right.

He couldn't remember feeling this way about another woman. Not even Madison. What he and his college girlfriend had shared wasn't like this. It had been immature and counterfeit.

Ever since Madison, he'd pushed women away. Assumed that his arthritis would always be a hindrance to a relationship. To marriage. But Emma treated him like he was normal and, for that, he was thankful.

He sighed and focused on the black, smoking structure in front of them.

The family store profits were integral to Emma's income and since she insisted on being self-reliant, he wasn't sure what she'd do to stay on top of her bills.

A fire truck pulled into the driveway and Emma turned from him to watch. The vehicle veered to the right into an unused pasture around the hoard of trucks in the drive. The firefighters quickly got out, set up and turned their hoses on the building. But everyone knew it was a lost cause.

Their high-powered spray, a much stronger force than the garden hoses, put the flames out. But the damage had been done.

They were left with a charred outline of the original structure. And it reeked. The scorched smoke in the air stung his eyes.

Emma turned her face from the sight, clinging to Carter as a firefighter strode over to them. The older man, John, cast a somber expression at Carter.

"Emma?" He introduced himself to her. Carter had been in his small group at Bible study once before, and the man was a gentle soul. "I'm afraid this building is condemned. You are going to have to rebuild."

She gave the man a tearful nod and thanked him and his team for arriving so quickly, all the while disengaging herself from Carter. Was she embarrassed that Carter was comforting his wife?

She took a step away and his chest felt empty without her leaning against him. Emma's grieved expression broke his heart. He'd do anything to fix this for her. But what?

Early the next morning, before the triplets were awake, Emma stepped off her front porch, still in disbelief that the family store was gone. She moved toward the now-cool blackened structure.

The firefighters had wrapped yellow tape around it before they'd left and her brothers-in-law arrived yesterday evening to build a temporary fence of green webbing around the structure so the children didn't get too curious.

She breathed in and as the smoky smell hit her anew, tears filled her eyes. How would she pay for the next scheduled hospital payment now that the family store was gone? Or rather, the next four? Her chin quivered, but she refused to let the tears fall.

She was a strong woman. Independent. She could figure this out.

Gravel crunched as Carter walked her way.

She could do this. She could move forward. But how?

"That shed was Robbie's first project on this property." Her lip quivered at the memory. "He was so proud of it."

"Yes, he was. It was all he could talk about for months," Carter said in an affectionate tone.

She glanced at the front porch, where she'd stacked the frozen beef. Shortly after the firefighters had left, Silas Murray had arrived to pick up his product. Product she could no longer sell, which meant she'd not get any commissions on beef until her store was rebuilt. How long did it take to demolish and rebuild something? Probably months, she worried.

"You can store goat milk in your fridge," Carter said, a helpful lilt to his voice.

"I know, but what about everything else?" Before he could answer, she strode over to the goats and let herself into Prancer's pen. Now that her buck was all better, he was back in the boys' pen with Chewie. She wrapped her arms around Prancer's neck. "What am I going to do, boy?"

Right when her store had started to make a profit and she was on target to pay her bills, all her plans had fallen apart with this stupid fire. She mashed her cheek against Prancer's furry neck, taking comfort in Robbie's goat.

She inhaled the soothing scent of the farm and pressed her eyes closed. What could she do? The scene from the coffee shop, where Carter had discovered that she'd transferred personal debt to her business card came to mind. Her eyes popped open.

Yes! Now that her personal card was debt-free, maybe she could charge the next few hospital payments on the credit card. Once the store was rebuilt, she'd be back in business and probably only have to put two payments on the card. And with Prancer ready for breeding season, she was hopeful for lots of kids to sell in the spring.

A solution. But more debt.

The Triple C Ranch truck rolled into the driveway. She let herself out of the pen and went over to see what was going on.

Carter's brothers were moving her rocking chairs off the wide porch.

She stepped beside Carter. "What's going on?" she asked.

"You'll see."

After his brothers settled the chairs on the side of the house, they pulled a long folding table out of the truck, carried it onto the porch and set it upright.

"What's that for?"

"A makeshift family store. You and the baker can still sell your product. The jam and relishes that have been selling so well can be brought back," he said. "My mom came up with the idea."

He looked at her with such excitement in his eyes that she couldn't help but fall into his waiting embrace. It felt wonderful to have him and his family there for her. A little jolt of pleasure shot through her as his arms wrapped around her waist. The fabric beneath her fingertips was soft and comforting. But then shame filled her at her growing attraction.

Appalled at herself, she jumped away from Carter like she was doing something wrong by allowing her husband to hold her. She had to get herself together and stop these emotions from steamrolling over her.

"I need a moment to myself, okay?" Without waiting for a reply, she turned and rushed to the safety of the back porch, where no one could see her fall apart. Her limbs shook as she allowed herself a good cry.

All she wanted was to grieve the family store that Robbie had worked so hard on. Instead, she couldn't think straight.

The blackened shell of the building caught her eye. If she had learned one thing from the fire, it was that all things come to an end. And nothing lasts forever.

Chapter Twelve

While the children were napping the next day, Carter stared at the charred remains of the family store he'd come to care so much about. His gaze swept over Jubilee Farm. The goats, the chickens, the dogs and the big dreams Emma had to make this place so much more.

As an accountant, he was more of a planner than a dreamer, so when Emma spouted off creative ideas, he respected how she thought outside of the box and envisioned an expanded homestead.

He still needed to discuss the credit card balance transfer, but today was not ideal.

Maybe another time when she wasn't so upset.

Emma trudged down the front steps, her gaze set off in the distance, almost a shell of the woman she was before the fire.

He fisted his hands and strode over to the goat pens, wishing he could make her feel better. "Sorry I've been MIA today, but work got crazy busy. I have a couple minutes right now if you need me to do anything."

"Thanks, but I..." Her response trailed off as his mother's truck glided into the driveway. Emma's eyes brightened at the sight and she didn't bother to finish her statement. Instead, she turned and raced into his mother's arms, who seemed to have become her mentor.

The day of the fire, his mother had been here to care for the triplets. But yesterday and this morning she'd been consumed with her summer camp, unable to come over. Seemed like his mother's presence might be exactly what Emma needed right now.

He freshened the water tubs while keeping an eye on the women. Maybe his mother could snap Emma out of the funk she was in. Emma was a strong fighter and the biggest optimist he knew, but the past few days she'd acted defeated and somber, like she was grieving.

She and his mother moved to the porch, then snapped a white tablecloth covered in red hearts over the folding table, transforming the porch into a cozy place to shop. How had his mother done that?

Emma gave his mother a quick hug.

The two of them moved the three-tier display cases that the baker from Love Valley had dropped off earlier, full of treats, back to the table, arranging them just so. One of the displays was full of cake pops and mini cupcakes Emma had made while she was up half the night. A tray on top of the kitchen fridge held the other half in case she sold out. The two smaller displays had a fresh supply of pecan pie and red velvet cake.

Emma stepped back and gave the miniature shop a once over and then clapped, a genuine smile covering her face. The first he'd seen since the fire.

He joined the happy pair. Emma looked over at him and gave a nod. His heart lifted that maybe her optimism was back, or at least clawing to return.

Just then, a white delivery truck pulled into the drive, closely followed by the cattle rancher who supplied Emma with beef to sell at her store.

"What in the world?" Emma stepped off the porch to greet the Murrays. Silas Murray must have said something exciting because Emma reached out to hug the extreme introvert. She stepped back, her hands clasped together in front of her as though she were about to burst with excitement.

The delivery truck driver hopped out, slid open the back, pulled a ramp into place and then disappeared inside the truck bed.

Before long, the delivery man was rolling a brand-new deep freezer down the ramp. Emma and the Murrays joined him as he rolled it to the side of the house near the front porch. An area that remained shaded all day long.

Emma was thanking Silas, and the man looked so uncomfortable that Carter felt sorry for him. "I just want my beef sold is all," Silas gruffly stated, but Carter couldn't miss the warmth in his eyes. Yes, he wanted his beef sold but, more importantly, he wanted to support Emma and her business. That was what their sweet town of Serenity was all about.

Carter's phone pinged with a meeting reminder, so he left the merry scene and slipped into the RV.

A few hours later, as he stepped out of the RV and rolled his stiff shoulders, he saw Autumn and Wyatt in the back field. They were playing with the triplets, the guard dogs and Autumn's precious Jack Russell terrier, Baby. It looked like they were playing chase. Or tag. He chuckled. They were doing something that would surely exhaust the children and give them a good night's sleep.

Emma strolled down the few porch steps with Esther Woodward. "You have saved the day," Esther told Emma. "And I'll get this cookie sheet back to you ASAP." She placed a packed tray of mini cupcakes on the floorboard of her truck and the two red velvet cakes the baker from Love Valley had brought over. "The ladies at the church tea are going to be thrilled with these baked goods."

He stepped beside Emma as the older lady drove off. "I can't believe I'm still in business." She turned to him, her eyes full of hope instead of despair. "I don't even have a functioning structure and I made good money today."

At least she'd likely be thrilled with the refrigerator Carter had finagled from a friend that would be delivered later and installed in her front hall. But since she had an aversion to him fixing things, he'd reserved judgment until his buddy showed up.

"By the way, when Autumn arrived, she and Wyatt did a quick inspection of Bear and Roxy," she said. "They feel the dogs are ready to fully guard." His stomach dropped. Now she'd expect him to move back to his bungalow because that had been the deal. He'd stay in the RV until the dogs were trained.

Except, he really enjoyed being a part of everyday life on Jubilee Farm. Helping with chores in the morning, sharing secret looks with Emma, watching the triplets grow, eating dinner with them as a family of five, putting the children to bed every night, and the list went on.

"I guess I can move back to town," he said, dreading the thought.

She placed her palm on his elbow and he wanted to reach for her dainty fingers.

He yearned to hold her hand, but he held back, unsure of what was happening between them. What if his attraction to her was growing simply because they lived on the same property? He wasn't sure, but he didn't want to fan the flames.

"What would people think? I mean—" she hurried on as though she was afraid if she didn't speak her mind that she'd lose the nerve "—other than your family, no one knows we have a marriage of convenience. Maybe it'd be best if you stayed here. For looks and all." She blushed.

Her words brought him more joy than he ever could have imagined. "Sure. The RV works fine for me."

She seemed relieved that he was willing to remain on the property. Did she want people to believe they were really married or did she actually like having him around?

"The RV can't be very comfortable, Carter. My offer of the guest room still stands."

"Thanks. I'll think about it."

He didn't care if he slept in the RV or the guest room. He just wanted to stay right here, where the first person he saw every morning was Emma, and the last person he saw before he settled in for the night was his adorable wife.

Laughter lifted from the field and they both turned their attention to the happy children.

The charred structure caught his eye and he was glad the defeated Emma from yesterday had retreated.

"Thanks for helping with everything. I don't think I could have done this without you and your family." Her voice cracked with emotion at the end of her statement.

"My pleasure." And it was. The somberness of the fire had seemed to draw the two of them closer together. Sure, it had taken over a day, but they'd finally found their rhythm again.

She finger-combed her hair and then slid the elastic band from her wrist into her hair. When she was done, she shook her head to make sure the ponytail was secure.

"The last few days have been wildly stressful. But now things seem like they're coming together." She pressed a palm to her chest. "I feel like I can breathe again."

Suddenly, he felt her head tip against his shoulder and he froze. When she let out a happy little sigh, he tried to stuff down his elation that she was leaning on him again, literally.

He swung his arm over her shoulder and she settled against his chest, a perfect fit. For a moment, it felt good. Right.

Then his stomach churned at the turn of events.

When Carter had proposed this marriage of convenience, he'd naïvely thought his emotions wouldn't be involved. He'd been so wrong.

"My lady," Carter said as he gestured for Emma to enter the coffee shop ahead of him. She giggled and did her best to prance through. It felt wonderful to see her happy, at least for a moment. The fire had been five days ago and so sudden they were both still in a state of shock. But the worst part had been Emma's sadness the first few days. Hopefully, that was behind them.

This felt like a date, exactly what he had hoped. Back when he'd told his mother about the marriage of convenience, she'd told him she was confident they'd fall in love. He had disagreed with her. But now hoped his mother's prediction would come true.

Emma snagged stools under the narrow live-edge wood counter that overlooked the sidewalk and, after he'd ordered, he joined her. He tossed her a grin because this time, away from the farm and responsibilities, was all about Emma. He wanted to give her a break from interruptions to… dream. Dream about the future of her successful family store.

And since the family store was doing

well and she'd exceeded her financial goal, he would not bring up the credit card balance transfer. She was much too independent to accept help from him. Anyway, it seemed like she had a plan to pay off the debt within the next six months. Though he'd have handled the situation differently, he decided to let the topic go. He had access to her business account and he'd make sure the balance was paid in full after the spring kids were successfully sold. If she still had an outstanding balance then, he'd bring it up.

She smiled at him, but it didn't quite reach her eyes. Probably thinking about the fire again. "Thank you for this respite. You understand how it feels having triplets. Seems I can never sit still if I'm home."

"Of course. Anytime."

"With the size of your family, there's no end to the babysitters you can call on." Her features held a wistful look. Or was that just sadness over the fire again?

Today, she sported fashionable capri pants that hugged her knees and a crisp white T-shirt, highlighting her summer tan.

"Oh, I've done my share of free babysitting in my day, so lots of favors to call in."

"That is so nice." The wistful look deepened to longing. Oh, that was definitely about how she grew up in an orphanage. He was able to decipher so much more about her changing features after a month and a half of marriage. But what she didn't understand was the McCaws were her family now, too. Maybe one day she'd realize that. Embrace them.

The barista delivered their coffees and Emma's trademark seven-layer bar.

Emma eyed her dessert with pleasure and then she frowned. "I can't stop thinking of the charred remains of the family store."

"My brother is going to bulldoze it tomorrow. Well, not bulldoze. Ethan and my dad have a skid steer with a grapple, so they'll remove the structure and leave the foundation intact."

Her eyes lit up. "Really?"

"Yup. I got a text message a little while ago that they have the time and equipment and would like to tackle the task first thing in the morning. If that works for you, we just need to order a dumpster."

They worked out the details and then Carter called a family friend who promised to drop the dumpster off this afternoon and pick it back up after the work had been completed.

She took a nibble of her sweet treat. "Even though I don't like the look of the structure anymore, it'll be even more sad after it's gone."

They both stared out the plate-glass window at the Serenity residents milling about on the sunny July day. Almost August. A group of teenage girls to their left began a fit of giggling.

She leaned back. "So, everything is set with insurance. I received the final approval yesterday afternoon. They will cover rebuilding what I had. I found the receipt from my older model refrigeration unit, so I just need to find a comparable used model somewhere." She sighed. "Which won't be easy because Robbie searched high and low for the one we bought."

He asked how much they were allocating for the refrigeration unit. She told him and he grinned.

"So, I found one," he said as he pulled out his phone to bring up the screenshot he'd taken of the gently used unit. "It's a year old and the owner is upgrading. I explained about the fire and he told me he'd hold it for you until noon today."

Her eyes widened when she saw the picture. "It looks like it's twice the size of the one I had before."

"That's about right. And it has tons of shelving, so you can have lots of shelves. Flip to that next shot."

She did and her mouth opened in an *O*.

"You want me to tell him you're interested in purchasing?" Her obvious excitement over the appliance thrilled him.

Her shoulders deflated. "No. I can't afford it."

"It's just a little more than what you told me the insurance company allocated to replace your refrigeration unit." He then named the amount the man was asking for the unit.

"Really?" At his nod, she jumped up and threw her arms around him and hugged tight. He could smell the citrus and vanilla shampoo she used and a hint of the coffee she'd been drinking. The moment felt frozen in time and he couldn't help but notice her lips were so close. In fact, if he moved his head just a little, he could kiss her.

Would she want that? Before he could put any more thought into the matter, she pulled away and settled on the stool beside him. What was he thinking? She was Robbie's girl. She was probably just excited about the deal he'd scoped out for her.

"I'm sorry," she said. "I shouldn't have thrown myself at you like that." She focused on her huge ceramic coffee mug and then glanced at him. But what he spotted in her eyes made him believe she wasn't sorry at all.

His pulse kicked up a notch. Could she be interested in him romantically? He was beginning to question his absolute aversion to letting another woman into his heart. Because if ever the woman existed who could break down his reserves, it just might be Emma Bailey.

He tried to tamp down his excitement over this development and scrambled to get their conversation back on track.

"These past few days I've been thinking about how we're going to rebuild the family store and it occurred to me that we don't need to rebuild it exactly how it was before." He cleared his throat, trying to dislodge the lump of emotion leftover from the enticing hug.

"But—"

"I think we have an opportunity here. And you should dream of what type of space will work for what you'd like the new and improved family store to accomplish."

"I'm firm on the budget."

"And I get that. As an accountant, I appreciate your fiscal awareness. But as your husband, I'm asking you to spend a few minutes dreaming about what you'd do different if you could." Had he just said *husband* out loud? Heat climbed up his neck and he fumbled with taking a sip of piping-hot coffee to cover his blunder.

First, he thought he spotted interest in her eyes and now he was throwing around the term "husband." Oh, he had it bad.

Part of him thought he shouldn't walk down that path. The safer route was to stay in the friend zone because he didn't want to get hurt again.

The other part of him craved sweeping his lips across hers to see her reaction.

But then what?

***

Emotions Emma couldn't place crossed over Carter's face. Maybe he was just as surprised as she that he'd used the term "husband." Of course, he was her husband, so why had the acknowledgment surprised them?

He focused on his phone and she on her yummy seven-layer bar as though he hadn't uttered that word.

From here, the appealing scent of his aftershave wafted over. Sometimes, in the evening after he'd left the house for the RV, she could still smell him on the couch. One night last week, she hadn't been able to leave the lingering scent and she'd slept right there on the couch, embarrassed when she'd woken up there in the morning with a crick in her neck.

He'd solidified a place in her heart a few days ago when the refrigerator he had borrowed from a friend arrived and was installed near the front door. It had made her temporary store complete and would allow her to continue making money so she could pay her bills on time. She'd be forever thankful to Carter for his unending thoughtfulness.

What had she been thinking when she'd thrown herself at him a little while ago? From day one, he had made it clear he wasn't interested in a relationship with anyone. Nor was she. Well, maybe she was just a tiny bit. But, hopefully, that little show of affection wouldn't make things awkward between them.

Carter slid his phone onto the wood counter. "Anyway, we could make the family store a different size," he said. "Add more windows. Maybe add a porch, even a covered porch. What are you thinking?"

That felt wrong. "You know how much work Robbie put into that structure. I want it built precisely like it was before the fire." Anything else might offend Robbie's memory.

"I disagree," Carter stated. "Robbie would jump at the opportunity to change things up. Yes, he was proud of the work he had done, but he was working with a sub-par existing structure. At least, that's what Robbie called it. He told me it wouldn't be big enough to serve your purposes, but it would have to do."

She vaguely recalled him telling her that as well. A couple of bistro tables would be nice, but they'd never fit in the old space. Anyway, to honor Robbie, she wanted to build it back exactly how it had been.

Then she remembered her quiet time these past few days and how God was impressing on her that it was time to let Robbie go. The fire had felt like a symbol for her to move on. She'd never forget Robbie. Hopefully, her children wouldn't, either. But she was much too young to cling to his memory for the next fifty years, if God gave her that much breath.

"Hey," Carter said as he touched her fingers ever so briefly. Even though it didn't last long, she enjoyed the moment. "You okay?"

She looked at Carter and her throat tightened. Here her husband was trying to get her to dream, as he called it, and she was living in the past. Well, no more!

"Yes, I'm good. Really good." She shifted forward and her knees lightly tapped Carter's. It felt good to be connected, if only by their knees. She had to trust her husband. He was a smart man. "You're right. I'm ready to rethink the store."

"What are you thinking?"

"I've always wanted a couple of bistro tables." She heard the hope and desperation in her voice. "But the space is too small."

Then he told her about the concrete bid he'd gotten to frame an identical eight-by-twelve section of foundation, which would effectively double her square footage.

"Well, I expect doubling the space means it would cost a lot more to rebuild the structure. But regardless, the insurance won't pay for it and I don't have any spare funds." For the moment, she ignored that third looming hospital payment.

"True. But if we cut costs in other areas, you'll have insurance money to pay for the concrete work."

This was all happening so fast, but if she were honest with herself, she'd always dreamed of a larger space. Somewhere ladies could congregate to fellowship. Many residents lived a good fifteen minutes from Serenity, so to have somewhere outside of town might be a draw. She'd provide a space to meet with one another and they'd purchase her products. A win-win.

She gazed into Carter's trusting face. He was smart, determined and an idea man. She admired him.

"As long as you can help me cut the budget somewhere else, I'd love to have the concrete work done. You know how I am with numbers." Then she thought about Carter's usual modus operandi. "But that doesn't mean you are going to pay for it."

She wagged her finger at him and they chuckled.

"I'll keep an eye on the budget, I promise. Leave the numbers to me. Anyway, I have an idea." Carter's dimpled smile came out to play.

"You are not paying for this, Carter." Except, for the first time, she almost hoped that was his plan because it felt like their relationship had developed. As though they were a team and she was finally okay with that. While she waited for him to explain, she got a little lost in his eyes. Flecks of caramel and dark brown swam in that chocolate sea.

"Nope. I've set up a workday, call it a barn raising, or a family store raising, but the town is planning to come to the property in two weeks and rebuild for you. We just need to knock out the details so we can order the supplies."

If her chin could drop to the ground, it would have. "Are you kidding me?" She felt dizzy with the thought of the town rallying around her.

She'd grown up unwanted, so she'd turned to books and her imagination. One book she'd read repeatedly had the townspeople come to the property after a tornado to rebuild the house. It was so sweet and full of community, and she loved the thought of people caring that much about others. She never realized it happened in real life.

And this time, she'd be the recipient.

She swallowed around the emotional lump in her throat, willing herself not to cry at the gracious offer. "Wow. Just wow. Robbie would be so thankful that Serenity is standing behind me." Carter blurred before her.

She had never felt as cherished as she did right now. She longed to reach for Carter and hug him, but one accidental and embarrassing hug a day was her maximum.

They may have nailed down the plan for rebuilding the family store, but their time together had left her longing for a deeper relationship with him. Her stomach quivered at the notion. She was feeling more than friendship for him, and she wasn't quite sure what to do with these new emotions.

Plan drawn, they left the shop and she settled in the passenger seat of his sedan. He held each side of the doorframe and leaned in. With him so near, his unique woodsy smell permeated the space, and she liked it. "You feel better about the future of the family store?" he asked.

Any stress left over dropped from her shoulders. "Oh yes. What with the temporary store you and your family helped me create on the front porch and now this?" She pointed at the paper where he'd doodled the new dimensions for the rebuild. "I'll be able to cover the rest of those scheduled payments."

Carter leaned back, surprise covered his face. "What payments? Is this something to do with the credit card balance transfer?"

Her stomach bottomed out at her loose tongue. She'd forgotten she hadn't told him. "I negotiated Addie's hospital stay into six equal payments. I have four payments left, but don't worry, I'm pretty sure I'm on track."

His nostrils flared as he stared at her and a slew of emotions crossed over his face. "And you didn't trust me enough to share that?"

Dread cut through her midsection at her blunder. She should have told him.

"I guess I didn't want you to fix things by paying it off for me," she whispered. Saying the truth out loud made her sound childish. Worse yet, the hurt covering his face shook her. She ran a shaky hand through her hair, wishing she hadn't been so secretive about her finances.

He was now her best friend. In fact, she had more than a surface attraction for him. What had started out as a simple marriage of convenience had turned into more. Much more.

To her surprise, she now felt united with Carter. And here she'd blown it because she'd tried to be Miss Independent. She blew out a breath, a stray lock of hair lifted.

"Emma, all you had to do was inform me about the negotiated payments and then ask me not to meddle. It pains me that you didn't realize I would have respected your wishes." He stepped back on the sidewalk, putting distance between them. "That you kept this secret from me. Well, it hurts." He placed his hand over his heart and the motion broke her.

He was right. They were married. He'd proven she could lean on him and was trustworthy.

Carter rounded the car, and she prayed she hadn't blown her chance at them turning into more than friends.

He settled in his seat, fired up the engine, then turned the air conditioning vents toward her warm face. Fast cooling air blew on her sweaty cheeks.

Even in the midst of hurting, Carter thought of her first. She blinked back sudden moisture at his constant kind ways.

"I don't get it, Emma. I thought we were partners." He stared straight ahead, not at her. The pain radiating from his features gutted her.

"We are, Carter. We are." She reached for his arm and he covered her hand with his own.

Had this stupid secret jeopardized whatever was blossoming between them? Worry churned in her gut. She hoped not, because even though she hadn't planned it, she might very well be falling in love with Carter McCaw.

Chapter Thirteen

The sun had risen a little while ago and Carter and his brothers had just finished setting up a tent they had borrowed from their church. Residents from the community would be here at any moment to help rebuild the family store.

It had been two weeks since the coffee date where he and Emma had reimagined her family store. That was also the day he'd discovered she'd been keeping a secret from him about the negotiated hospital bill. Though she had hurt him, she had apologized. And from how well they'd been working as a team since then, he figured she'd just been afraid to trust him. Now that the secret was out in the open, they'd put the deception behind them and their relationship was progressing. Truth be told, he was falling in love with Emma. He only hoped she felt the same toward him.

His brother and father had removed the old structure. The concrete guy had framed and poured a fresh slab of concrete, so the new area was now more than double the space of the original store. Carter had made the executive decision to add the porch. It'd be easier to do it now rather than add it later on. He hoped Emma would understand.

"Hey, Steve," Walker said. "You can set up your circular saw under the tent."

"Let me plug this extension cord in," Carter said as he unwound a lengthy industrial power cord looped around his arm and plugged it into the electrical outlet beside Emma's front porch. Where was she, anyway? He had figured she'd be out before sunup, but he hadn't seen her yet. In fact, right as he was about to go into the kitchen to get coffee, his brothers had arrived and given him the caffeine he'd so desperately needed. Darn, he'd wanted a glimpse of Emma drinking her morning coffee and settling the children before their big day. Seemed she was always on his mind lately. He tried to wipe the goofy grin off his face before someone noticed and gave him a hard time.

A white extended-cab pickup truck pulled into the gravel drive and squeezed in next to the RV. Everyone was trying to park as far away from the job site as possible so the volunteers would have space to work. Doc Earl and his whole Bible study group emerged from the vehicle. A smile tipped Carter's lips as he offered the men a wave.

Already sweating, he ducked under the food and drink tent to snag a cup of water.

"Is one of the triplets crying?" Ethan

asked, his head cocked toward the little brick one-story house.

Carter turned his head and heard what sounded like Addie wailing. He rushed to the house. The closer he got, the more he was convinced Mikey was in on it as well. He punched in the security code to unlock the door and pushed into the house.

As he crossed the threshold, he heard all three children wailing like never before. Almost like they were in pain. He rushed to open their bedroom door. Tears were streaming down their red faces. He crouched on the ground and they scrambled to him, almost tipping him over as they clung to his neck.

Where was Emma?

Maybe, more importantly, was something wrong with her?

Panic thrummed through him at the thought.

He held tight to the children and talked softly to soothe them. His heart splintered that they'd needed someone and he'd been outside, oblivious to their distress. He felt like a horrible father, but tried not to chide himself too harshly since Emma hadn't asked for his help.

When they'd finally calmed down, he let Mikey crawl onto his back, which was awkward with his cast, but he succeeded. Then Carter put each girl on a hip. Leaving their bedroom, he glanced down the hall at the room he knew was Emma's, but the door was shut tight. His unease over her welfare grew as he made his way to the other end of the house. Mikey was trying to kick him and get him to gallop like a horse, but with three healthy three-year-olds clinging to him, his primary goal was to get them into the kitchen and secure the safety gate.

His mother entered the home, shutting and locking the door behind her. With three toddlers, safety was always at the top of everyone's mind.

"Look at you," his mother said. "You look like a monkey carrying all those children."

When he got to the kitchen, he knelt to let them down. His mother had a point. He'd actually sat on the floor with the children with much less joint pain than a couple of months ago. And carrying all three? A month ago, he'd thought that'd be impossible. But with his diet change, supplements, collagen and now working with a personal trainer twice a week, something was making him more limber and flexible. Probably not like other men his age, but much better than before.

"Where's Emma?" his mother asked.

He briefly explained what he had walked into, so his mother said she'd check on his wife.

As his mother left the kitchen, closing the baby gate behind her, Carter turned to the triplets. "Who's hungry?"

Three chubby hands shot up. Quickly, he poured three watered-down juices into sippy cups and settled each child into their booster seat with a drink. Then he fetched a container of cleaned blueberries and gave them each a handful to munch on while he cracked some fresh eggs.

His mother stepped over the gate and sidled up next to him. "Emma is boiling hot. I'm going to put some soup on for her, grab her some water and juice, and rummage through her bathroom for pain reliever."

He reared back as he heard about his wife's ailment. She would be so disappointed to not be able to partake in today's festivities.

His mother patted his arm. "It's just a fever, probably a twenty-four-hour thing. But I've sent Esther a text. She's on her way over to help with the children and Emma today. She and I will stay in the house and take care of things in here while you boys build the new store for her."

A buzz sounded from the front door unlocking and Esther appeared. He'd never been so grateful for these two women before. With everything happening outside, he wasn't sure what he'd do if he was responsible for the triplets, Emma and building the new family store.

"Ambulance is here," someone outside yelled.

His heart raced as his gaze connected with his mother's and she said, "Go." Esther took over the egg cracking and he rushed to the front door to see what the emergency was. How could someone be hurt when they hadn't even started yet?

He scrambled out the door to see Lance, his Bible study leader and top paramedic, hop out of the ambulance in uniform and amble toward him.

"Thought, since we're a volunteer crew, that it'd be smart to have the ambulance here. But I'm ready to help build. What should I do?"

Relief flooded through Carter that there wasn't an injury and the ambulance was just a precautionary measure.

He glanced around and saw that most everyone they'd expected was already there, milling about. Emma would have been so excited to be a part of this. He prayed she felt better soon so she could take part, or at least see the town rallying around her.

But right now, he needed to gather everyone together and organize them into groups the way he and Ethan and Walker had planned the night before.

Hammering and sawing noises filled the air, but Emma could barely raise her head off the pillow let alone consider getting out of bed to partake in this exciting day. If she could just make it over to the window to see the progress, she'd be happy. But she couldn't move. Her eyes were scratchy and her arms felt like lead weights. It broke her heart that the town had united to rebuild her family store and she couldn't even participate.

But right now, the sun seeping in around the edges of the closed blinds pierced her eyes like shards of glass. She shut her eyes and turned her head into the shadows for blessed relief.

Through the cacophony outside, she heard Carter's voice above everyone else's. Oh, he wasn't directing people. No, she could hear him encouraging others, praising their work and thanking them for being a part of this special day. Her throat tightened at his thoughtfulness. He probably knew she was disappointed she couldn't be out there, so he was trying to be the host, so to speak. Make sure everyone knew how much they were appreciated.

Shivering in bed, Emma felt so helpless. She couldn't go outside. Couldn't care for her children. She couldn't even care for herself. But Carter was out there representing her today. Her heart squeezed at his thoughtfulness.

She'd known him for six years. Met him the day she and Robbie had moved to Serenity. He had helped them unload their meager belongings from a U-Haul trailer. Today he was still a caring person who'd give the shirt off his own back.

And, really, wasn't that what he'd done

two months ago when he'd married her so the triplets could have medical insurance? He'd given up the chance to marry for love, just so his best friend's widow was taken care of. She'd be forever thankful to him.

"Mommy, Mommy," Addie cried out, but just as quickly she was pacified by either Cora or Esther. What would Emma have done without them today? Happy tears formed in Emma's eyes at the support system she had.

In reality, she'd probably had this support system when Robbie was alive, but she'd been too stubborn to open her eyes and see the gifts God had given her through the people of Serenity who cared about her. Especially the McCaw family who'd taken Robbie under their wing when he'd been an orphan in high school. He'd had so many family dinners at their home that, when she'd met him, she had no idea he'd come from such a broken background.

She'd been acting like she was defective

because her parents had dumped her in the foster care system and never come back for her, but in reality, Emma was a whole person. Someone who had lived through a tough experience and had learned a great deal about herself.

The hammering and nailing and joking voices put a smile back on her face as she drifted off to sleep.

A click woke her. She opened her eyes feeling much more refreshed than she had earlier. Carter stood there, Stetson in hand, hair messed up and sweat creasing his brow. He had never looked more handsome.

She tried to give him a smile, but it probably looked like a grimace.

His eyes lit up, so she must have somewhat succeeded in her smile. "Feeling better?" he whispered.

She tried to shrug but wasn't sure if her shoulder lifted or not. He stepped into the room.

"Is it okay if I'm in here? My mom

said…" His voice trailed off as he twirled his cowboy hat in that nervous expression he had.

She wiggled her fingers at him in a "come here" gesture. "Of course you can. How are things going out there?" Two months ago, relying on him for this workday would have driven her crazy. But she had grown to trust him over these past few months, and he'd done an admirable job planning for today. To complete the project before sunset, he'd even scheduled an electrician and finagled the guy who did building inspections to attend the workday. Carter was a gem.

He knelt next to the bed and leaned over with his phone. "Since you can't be out there, I wanted to give you a visual update."

Nerves fluttered in her stomach. She wasn't sure if it was because of his nearness or the excitement at seeing what was happening out there.

"Be forewarned. It isn't much yet, but I

knew you'd be antsy to see," he said as he tapped the photo icon.

She sucked in a breath. Her family store was framed in. Moisture collected in her eyes at the fresh look filling the space.

She watched and listened as he flipped through each photo and explained what was happening and told all the funny stories about things that had happened so far today.

"Sounds like everyone is being productive and having a great time."

"They are." He kept flipping, but something looked off. Almost like someone had measured wrong.

"What's that? Will that section be finished soon?" Hadn't he said the rough-in framing was complete?

He pointed to the section she was worried about. "So, that's the porch. It'll have an overhang. The triplets will be in school soon enough and then you'll have the space for people to come in for pre-prepared sandwiches or maybe coffee or sweet tea or lemonade. Just like you wanted."

"But we didn't plan that porch space." And how'd it get there? She'd seen the concrete slab that had been poured. Was she missing something? She didn't want this porch to cut into the interior space she was counting on.

"It's my birthday gift to you," Carter whispered. Her birthday was in two weeks. Her heart hitched at his sweet motivation.

"That's too much. You can't build someone a porch for their birthday. No," Emma said sternly, as though he was a triplet who wouldn't share. She couldn't accept this extravagant gift, could she? But the warmth spreading through her core had nothing to do with her fever and everything to do with her readiness to accept such an overwhelming offering.

"It's done." He gave her a crooked and nervous grin. "Happy birthday."

She glanced at the photo again and could clearly see a wide porch beyond the door. "How wide is it?"

"It runs along the entire front of the store

and is four feet deep." His dimples flashed at her and she pressed her lips together in an attempt to keep the grateful tears from falling. He looked embarrassed to be gifting her something so extraordinary. Something she'd use every day for years to come, and think of him with each use.

"And the inside of the store is still sixteen by twelve." He nodded. The tension in her shoulders released when he confirmed the dimensions had not changed. Better yet, he hadn't thrown money at a problem. He'd thought long and hard about getting her a birthday gift that she'd use and be grateful for.

"Thank you, Carter. I think I'm going to love that porch." He was right. The triplets would be in school soon enough and she'd always dreamed of expanding her offering. And it made sense to do it now, while the building was under construction.

She covered his hand with hers and gazed into his sparkling eyes. What she saw in the depths spoke of something that had once scared her. But now, she welcomed. "That just might be the nicest birthday gift I've ever received." Carter caressed the back of her hand with his thumb, sending warmth down her arm.

His touch comforted her as her eyes felt heavy with sleep.

If she wasn't sure over these past few days, she was positive now—she had fallen in love with her husband.

And if she had to guess, his feelings toward her were growing as well.

Grinning, she drifted off to sleep.

Carter could tell the moment Emma fell asleep. The cute worry lines between her eyebrows softened and her giddy smile over the surprise front porch slackened.

A few minutes ago, when her hand had covered his, it had sparked to life feelings he'd been trying to ignore. When Emma had looked at him, he'd felt hopeful. He'd felt whole.

He wasn't sure when he'd fallen in love with his wife, but he had.

And this wasn't anything he'd ever felt before. This feeling was powerful and not to be ignored.

Even though there was much to do, he couldn't bring himself to leave her side. Not now. The warmth from her hand was intoxicating.

In the past month, he'd turned into a sappy man, longing for his wife to reach for him and gaze at him with a look of tenderness.

What had the earlier look of affection meant to her? Was she just happy about the covered porch or was she falling for him as well? Maybe she was just grateful for the progress on the family store. It was possible he shouldn't read anything into this.

Or...could his greatest dream be coming true?

He was already father to three sweet children. But could he also be a real husband to the woman he now loved?

A soft knock and a simultaneous push on the door had him untangling his hand from Emma's and stumbling to stand. His mother peeked into the room and whispered, "How's the patient?" Except, by the expression in her eyes, Carter could tell she'd seen their hands intertwined. Saw him leaning over the bed staring at Emma with adoration.

He cleared his throat as he stood and pushed the chair back from the bed. "Good. I showed her pictures of the progress. But then she fell asleep."

His mother nodded, but she had a knowing look in her eyes, so he hightailed it out of there and joined the men working on the siding, where it was safer.

His mind traveled back to the day he and Emma had said their wedding vows two months ago. They'd been friends and he'd known her pretty well, but since that day Emma and the triplets had become his world. Sure, he still worked as an accountant, had meetings, had even received a promotion and a raise since their wedding day, but his life had changed so much. Besides God, Emma was now the most important person in his life. Other than the eight hours he worked every day, they spent every moment together. He'd gotten a chance to know her better. Seen her when she was frustrated and angry, and he adored how she handled what life threw at her.

At first, they'd been good friends, then grown into confidants, then best friends. That was probably when his attraction toward her began to grow. And now he was in love. He only prayed she felt the same.

Later that day, after the electrical was complete and inspected, the roof and siding were installed, he took more pictures to show Emma. She was going to be shocked at the amount of work they'd completed so far, and they were on task to complete the store before sundown.

With his hand on her bedroom door and the triplets chattering away in the playroom with his mother and Esther, the moment from earlier played in his mind and he smiled.

But then he wondered what would happen if he revealed that he loved her and she didn't feel the same? He shuddered. That would crush him.

He shook his head. No. They were married. Committed. Even if she never loved him like he loved her, they would still remain married. Anyway, Emma would never dismiss him with cruel words like Madison had.

He gave a soft knock before slipping into her room. She was fitfully sleeping, so he raked his hand through his messy hair and frowned. His chest ached that he would not be able to see her reactions to the new pictures.

When he turned to leave, she whispered Robbie's name. He cocked his head. Maybe he'd misheard. He twisted back. Her eyes were closed, and she said Robbie's name one more time, louder this time.

His heart sank at the implication of that

one word. He slipped out of the room and leaned against the casing for support. He thought his legs might collapse under him as he processed what she had just said.

Even though he was confident in his feelings for her, what just happened made him realize she would never, could never, care for him like she had Robbie. Robbie had been her one true love and nothing would change that.

He took a fortifying breath, pocketed his phone with the exciting pictures and strode out to the work site. Emma didn't love him and never would.

The air smelled heavy of cut lumber, earthy and warm. Their volunteer crew had worked hard today. The structure was almost complete. He glanced back at the house. He had been so excited earlier at Emma's showing of affection. But after hearing her late husband's name on her lips, he was troubled.

This love story would not end the way Carter had hoped.

After hearing Emma's true feelings, he wasn't sure he could keep going on as if nothing had happened. He'd love to move back to his place in downtown Serenity. He could use his steam shower again and, after today, that would feel wonderful. He could sleep on his soft queen-size mattress that he'd missed so much. He could even dine out every night like he had as a bachelor. But if he moved back to his bungalow, the townspeople would talk. And neither he nor Emma wanted that.

The one thing he knew was that he could not keep living here and acting as though things were fine, when in fact everything had changed.

How could he step away from Emma without the world finding out?

She still loved her late husband, probably always would. What could Carter say or do to change her mind? Nothing. Absolutely nothing. Her heart belonged to Robbie.

Chapter Fourteen

The next day, Carter let himself into the house, strode to the playroom and peeked around the corner. Laney, his sister-in-law, had sent him a text message alerting him that Emma had gone to her room to nap. Sure enough, Laney, her one-year-old and the triplets were the only people in the room. As he stepped over the baby gate, Mikey spied him.

"Papa C," he cried out. That caught the girls' attention and they all came running, clamoring for his attention. He settled on the floor in front of the train table to play with trains and snuggle.

Yesterday, after the workday had completed and everyone had left the job site, he'd sent his mother a text. He'd told her he'd be super busy at work over the next few days and because Emma was weak from this illness, could she send enforcements over to help until she recovered? His mother had replied right away. He could always count on his family. Then he'd gone to town and picked up some groceries and a meal from the diner, staying within the bounds of his anti-inflammatory diet.

"Lunch?" Mikey asked. The boy was always hungry. Carter couldn't imagine the grocery bills when he entered middle school.

"Not yet, buddy. Trains?" Mikey picked up two trains and started making vroom noises, as though he was trying to crash into Carter's train.

Carter beamed. He loved these children so much. After only a couple of months, he couldn't imagine going a day without connecting with them.

Cassie stood behind him, her arms around his neck, telling him some story about how Bear had knocked her over and given her a boo-boo. Sounded like a tall tale to him since Bear and Roxie were gentle souls and had never come close to hurting any of the children.

"Where?" Carter turned.

Cassie pushed her wrist at him. "Right there."

He pressed a kiss against the spot. "All better?" She grinned and nodded while Mikey vied for his attention.

Carter faced the train table and picked up a train car. His plan was to have breakfast and dinner in the RV and head over to his parents' for lunch. Since it wasn't uncommon for him to drop by for lunch, they wouldn't notice he was trying to avoid Emma. At least until his bruised heart healed some.

And for as long as people were helping

Emma, he'd drop by once or twice a day, whenever Emma was napping, to spend some quality time with the triplets.

His plan should work for a while. Except, at some point, he'd have to man up and allow things to return to normal around here. But there was no way to bottle up his romantic feelings toward Emma and pretend they didn't exist. Because they did.

Maybe a few days of not seeing her would help.

"I couldn't sleep," Emma stated as she stepped over the gate. His heart pitter-pattered at the sight of her. Even with dark circles under her eyes and dressed in baggy sweats and an oversized T-shirt, she was simply the most gorgeous woman he'd ever seen.

She looked his way and brightened. "Hey, we missed you this morning. Everything okay?"

"Yup. Just busy at work." He refused to make eye contact with her. It would hurt even more to see those sky-blue eyes and know he could never have her for himself.

He stood, amazed that his knees barely hurt and tousled Mikey's hair.

"In fact, I've got a meeting soon." He nodded at Laney and let himself out.

"Salmon for dinner," Emma called.

His heart hitched. He would absolutely not be here for dinner. Perhaps he should speak with Pastor Tony. Yes, Carter had agreed to a lifetime, but he never imagined feelings would be involved. Pastor Tony had told them that marriage was hard work. And that it was a choice.

Yes, Carter was living in the RV and choosing to stay. He even had a plan to spend quality time with the children.

But was he wrong to step away from Emma's life, even if only for a few days?

He closed the front door behind himself and pressed the key pad to lock the door.

This was the only thing he could do for the moment to protect his aching heart.

***

Emma still didn't understand why Carter had pulled away. Sure, when she was napping, he'd come all stealthlike to see the triplets. Obviously, he'd been working in cahoots with his sisters-in-law over the past few days. But after she'd interrupted his visit on the first day, she'd made a point to stay away when he was there. Something was amiss that he wasn't ready to talk about. She hadn't seen him for three days, other than their stilted and awkward exchange the day after the workday.

Three long gut-wrenching days.

And she missed him.

Had she said something to offend him in her sickened delirium? She didn't think so.

Out the kitchen window, she spotted the brand-new family store standing tall and proud after the town "barn raising." She couldn't believe she had been sick in bed while those sweet people had worked to help her. Tears pricked her eyes that the community had been here for her. That the McCaw siblings, led by Carter, had planned the entire event.

"Come back to the playroom, Emma." Autumn approached. "You look white as a ghost. I don't want you passing out." She wrapped her arm around Emma's waist and guided her to the couch in the sun-filled room.

The triplets' shrill screams and loud playing didn't make her head pound anymore, thankfully, but she was still weak from whatever bug had taken her down.

"Thanks for coming over today," Emma said.

She was so grateful to have people who cared. Carter's sisters-in-law had spent the past two days with her. Clearly, none of them thought she was stable enough to be left alone for long. And, frankly, the dizziness and fatigue left over from whatever bug she had caught before the workday didn't make her the best caregiver, so she was thankful.

Autumn had come over this morning to

do a wellness check on Bear and Roxy, and spent the day. Except Emma knew better; Autumn's decision to stay had been planned. The McCaws were concerned about Emma, especially because Carter was MIA. Emma settled back on the couch cushions, plotting her next question in an attempt to find out what was going on with Carter. His sister had to know more than she did.

"Have you seen Carter?"

Autumn pursed her lips together while Emma pulled the soft blanket up to her chin to ward off the chilly air-conditioning. "I stopped by the RV on my way in today and Carter was still in his pajamas just lazily drinking a cup of coffee and looking like a man who hasn't slept in a week." She grimaced. "He also looked like a guilty man when I asked why he wasn't over here. He rushed out some lame excuse, but there was something in his eyes I haven't seen since Madison broke up with him. Is there something going on that you're not telling me?"

Emma's stomach clenched at him being hurt like that all over again, but she couldn't remember anything out of the ordinary during that workday.

She shook her head. It didn't matter. He'd shown his true colors and abandoned her, just like her parents had. Better now than allowing their relationship to get more serious.

The night the family store had been completed, she'd expected Carter to stop in. Yes, it had been late. Cora had already fed and bathed the triplets then put them down for the night. Emma hadn't had the energy to make it to the front porch, but she'd watched from her window as Carter said goodbye to the last of the volunteers and then headed straight for the RV without a second glance back at her house. At first, she figured he'd wanted a shower, but then she'd fallen asleep and woken up a few hours later and no Carter. Convinced he'd come over but hadn't wanted to bother her, she'd checked her front porch camera, but no Carter. For some reason, he'd chosen not to reconnect with her that evening. And each day that had passed since, without his presence, her heart had felt heavy in her chest.

Somehow she'd grown to rely on him as much as she depended on air. But his comment the other day, when she'd come to the playroom unexpectedly, about being busy at work, had been short and to the point. She shivered at the memory of the businesslike exchange they'd had before he'd rushed away.

And now she was afraid he wouldn't be coming back at all, which was crazy because she was furious at him.

Yes, he'd lived up to the marriage bargain promise by adding the triplets to his medical insurance. He'd even remained in her RV in that cramped space. But now he wasn't spending any time with her or on the farm, though he'd made it a point to visit the triplets several times a day since the workday.

She had thought he'd enjoyed living on Jubilee Farm. Enjoyed being a rancher, albeit a goat rancher, a father, a friend, a confidant. She'd even thought they'd meant something to each other. That their relationship was turning into something more than friendship.

Her gut twisted at his absence.

"You miss him?" Autumn brought her out of her thoughts.

"I shouldn't, but I do." She sucked in a breath. Those two little words reminded her of their wedding ceremony. The day when she hadn't felt confident about saying those words. She had worried that marrying Carter would tarnish Robbie's memory.

But it hadn't. Just the opposite.

Marrying Carter had ignited her life. Started her living again and given her hope and a focus for the future.

Then he'd gone and ruined it by creating this huge chasm between them.

Now the future felt bleak without Carter beside her. Her throat clogged just thinking about going through each day without him by her side. Moisture filled her eyes. She blinked the wetness away.

"You love him, don't you?" Autumn's words were soft and gentle.

A tear trickled down Emma's face and she swiped it away. "He made life so much more fun, you know?" Her voice cracked as she wiped at her face again. She swallowed around the lump in her throat. In reality, she had been a happier person these past two months. Carter made life so much richer, just by being there. But he obviously didn't share Emma's romantic feelings. He only considered her a friend, if that.

"He always kind of annoyed me," Autumn joked, which broke the tense mood and made Emma chuckle. Siblings. She'd never had any, but she could tell the McCaw siblings loved each other fiercely.

She smiled at her friend's engagement with the children today. Emma didn't have the energy to move off this couch let alone play with the children, so she was grateful Carter's family had dived in.

Autumn strode across the room and slipped beside Emma. "I don't know what's happening in his head, but I know he adores you." She rubbed Emma's arm with a look in her eyes that reminded Emma how Autumn had recently almost lost the love of her life. But Autumn and Wyatt had worked it out. And now they were happily married and expecting a baby soon.

"I think Carter only sees me as Robbie's wife," she said, her chest tightened at her words. "Someone he promised to take care of."

Autumn straightened. "That's not true. I've seen the way Carter looks at you."

"You weren't here the other day. Now

things are awkward and stilted between us and I don't know why." In fact, he'd almost looked disappointed in Emma for something, but she had no idea what.

"Emma, he's crazy about you."

"You think?" At Autumn's firm nod, hope fluttered in her belly. Pastor Tony's words about how marriage was work flooded Emma's mind. How marriage was also about compromising.

She rolled his wise counsel over in her head. Maybe she should reach out to Carter. After all, he was the one who had given up his life and identity to marry her to provide her children with insurance.

She'd never thought she'd fall in love again. How good was God to give her not one love, but two?

Except, it didn't matter because Carter had emotionally left her, and he wouldn't have done that if he cared for her romantically.

"I'm going to my room to take a nap," she told Autumn. What Emma really needed was quiet time with God to sort all this out. To decide if she should be the one to make the first move.

Because even if Carter didn't love her, she still wanted him in her life.

How could he make his romantic feelings toward Emma go away? Carter shook his head in frustration and pulled into his parents' driveway wondering what his mother needed help with that couldn't wait until lunchtime.

He shook off his gloomy state of mind and trudged up the steps to the wide front porch. Was Emma enjoying her family store's new porch? Would she pick up those bistro tables she'd been eyeing at the consignment shop? Man, he missed her.

He pushed open the front door.

"In the kitchen," his mother called out.

Sweetness and cinnamon combined in the air. He followed the luscious smell to the back of the house.

A plate of oatmeal cookies sat at the

center of the table. His mother put the romance book she was reading down.

"Sit. Can I get you coffee?"

He stood, hands gripping the back of a chair. "Mom, I'm in the middle of a workday. What did you need help with that couldn't wait?" With her reading a book and acting all relaxed, he had a bad feeling about the reason she'd summoned him.

"I just need to understand why you are no longer spending time at Emma's."

"What does that mean? I live in the RV on her property."

His mother leaned forward. "Have a seat, son."

Carter gritted his teeth. An ambush, that's what this was. He scuffed a hand over his face. How had he not seen this coming?

He settled in the chair across from her, knowing how tenacious his mother was. If she had something to say, she'd say it, whether or not you liked it.

He had a feeling he wouldn't like where

this conversation was headed. Nor the challenge his mother would likely make.

Though, it wasn't anything he hadn't been beating himself up over.

He might as well let her get whatever she had to say off her chest. He met her steely gaze.

"So, why aren't you spending time with Emma?"

"I told you. Busy with work." Short and to-the-point. Answer nothing unasked. Exactly how you'd handle a police interrogation. It was the best way to deal with his mother.

She steepled her fingers and leaned her chin on them. "But you come over here for lunch. Take leftovers home. Have secret playtime with the triplets when Emma is napping. Spill."

He studied his mother. The lines on her face that she'd earned from loving hard and working hard. She adored him. Only wanted the best for him. And he'd been second-guessing himself for three days.

It might make sense to talk with someone about the situation. Someone who cared and would be honest.

So, he told her everything. How he'd fallen in love. How he thought maybe Emma might feel the same. But then, the day of the construction project, she'd said Robbie's name while she was dreaming, a smile covering her face.

"She'll always love him, Mom. I will never match up."

His mother pressed her back against her chair and lifted her chin. "You're right, she'll always love Robbie. He was her first love and the father of her triplets. She'll never forget him."

Carter's shoulders dropped. Just like he had thought. But it didn't help to have another woman confirm his worst fears. His torso constricted. How was he going to keep living each day with this insurmountable love in his heart for Emma? Would the sharp pain in his ribs lessen over time?

His mother intertwined her fingers in front of her. "I see how she admires you, son. It's not how she looked at you back when you married so the triplets could have health care. No. Back then, she appreciated you and considered you a friend, maybe even a good friend. But over the past few weeks, I've seen how she touches you. Peeks at you when you aren't paying attention. Oh boy, the depth of how she gazes at you, that's love if I've ever seen it."

"No," he stated, steadfast. "You weren't there that day. She was dreaming of Robbie. You don't do that when you love another man."

His mother firmly shook her head. "I know she loves you. Who knows, she may not know yet herself, but she does." She gave another nod for effect. "You need to go back to Jubilee Farm and talk with her. Integrate yourself back into her life. Into the triplets' lives."

"No, Mom, I can't—"

"You are a married man and that won't change," she said tightly. "You need to be a part of their lives. You've always dreamed of being a father and here's your chance. Those children miss you and want you in their lives. And you need them."

At the mention of the triplets, some of his composure cracked. He missed spending so much time with them, not just the stolen moments, but dinner and bedtime and joyous times. And he yearned to be with Emma once again.

Except, Carter wasn't sure how to spend day after day with a woman who pined for another man and would never reciprocate his affections.

"Even though Emma only asked you for medical insurance, you told me that you had promised Robbie to be a part of the triplets' lives. When this marriage of convenience came about, you shared it was a good way to keep your promise." Then she gave him that stern look of hers. "And Mc-Caws keep their promises. Regardless, in the book of James, God states that every good gift and every perfect gift is from above. Carter, God gave you Emma. Go, be her husband."

Her words about that verse hit him like a two-by-four. God had given Emma to him. Even if she didn't want a real marriage, she was a gift, as were the triplets. He couldn't walk out on them even if he was hurt.

His mother made a to-go baggie of the anti-inflammatory cookies for him and sent him on his way, like he was a teenager again.

Back in the RV, he spent the afternoon alternating between agreeing with his mother and wanting to lock himself in his bungalow in town for a month.

How could he reenter Emma's life after he'd up and walked away?

Did Emma even want him around?

The image of the triplets floated through his mind. His wild man, Mikey, who never stopped. Cassie, the happiest little girl unless she wasn't, and then she screeched so loud it sounded like a cat was being tortured. And sweet Addie, so tiny, but she was a pistol who stood her ground. He sighed. Did they miss him as much as he missed them?

Lord, You set this plan in motion months ago when You gave me the idea to propose a marriage of convenience. Did You know I'd fall in love with Emma? Carter rubbed the back of his neck where tension had gathered.

Why had he assumed he could marry Emma to give the children medical insurance and not fall head over heels in love with her? She was gorgeous and smart and one of the kindest women he'd ever met. Probably because he'd trusted that he was following God's will and that God would protect him.

But what if throwing him into the blender with Emma had been exactly what he'd needed to start living again? His office chair squeaked as he leaned back.

He knew God had provided him with the lifetime chance to be a father to the triplets, and he didn't want to mess up that opportunity. If he let go of his pride and knocked on her door to apologize, he'd be able to spend time with the triplets, tuck them into bed each night, be part of their special memories. But he wasn't sure he could do it because he'd be around Emma a lot. And now that he knew he loved her and she still ached for Robbie, being around her would be much too painful.

He pushed away from his computer, frustrated that he hadn't gotten a lick of work done since he'd returned from the Triple C.

Before he could think it over, he sent a text to Emma.

Free later on?

After what felt like an eternity, she replied. His chest pounded as he opened the message.

Sure. The triplets would love to see you. Dinner at 5?

His pulse raced at the text. He reread it but couldn't find any underlying message that *she* wanted to see him.

What if the triplets missed him but their mother didn't?

Frustrated, he headed for the shower, running his fingers over the weeklong scruff on his chin, as excitement over an evening with his favorite children and the woman he loved thrummed through him.

He had to trust that God hadn't given Emma to him just to bruise his heart. He needed to have confidence that the Lord had a plan to take care of Carter's emotions if Emma could never move on from Robbie. After all, He promised not to give His children more than they could handle.

He closed his eyes and envisioned Emma's sweet face. Her lyrical laugh. Her gentle approach to the children. Her steadfast trust in him.

Oh, who was he kidding? Even if God didn't protect his heart, Carter couldn't wait to drink in Emma's face again.

Chapter Fifteen

Emma didn't have time to prepare a special meal, but she figured having Carter over during the dinner hour would keep the adults busy, leaving little opportunity for private conversations. While the triplets were in their room napping, she was setting the table. With cloth napkins. Her throat clogged with emotion. Why was she trying so hard? He'd made his decision and deserted her. That spoke volumes.

His disappearance had scraped at her childhood wound of abandonment. Did his visit have anything to do with their relationship? Probably not. Carter likely just missed the children and the "favorite thing" dinner tradition.

Which was fine because her children needed him.

A quick glance at the clock showed she had a half hour before he'd arrive. She smoothed the front of her worn work shorts down. Why was she so nervous?

Tonight was about trying to mend their fractured relationship so the children could spend adequate time with Carter. And a half hour a day wouldn't cut it. Somehow, she and Carter needed to come to an agreement that worked for everyone. Starting with Carter explaining why he'd disappeared.

She rounded the table and put knives in two of the place settings. The table was set as it used to be when Carter was here for every meal. Her eyes teared up at the memory of the amazing meals they'd had around this table as a family of five. She yearned for those times back.

She pushed a lock of hair away from

her chin. Thankfully, she was feeling better. The visit with Autumn and her comments about Carter had seemed to bring Emma out of her daze. Made her realize this was her new normal, and she'd better stand strong in it.

When the children had taken an unexpected morning nap, so had she. She'd woken up refreshed and feeling better than she had in a while. She'd spent time alone in her bedroom praying about the situation and had come to a peace. The Lord pressed upon her heart that she needed to clear the air between them. Something had changed and she purposed to find out what. She prayed she could fix it because she longed for a future with Carter.

She hoped they could put this disagreement, or whatever had happened, behind them so she could enjoy the man God had placed her with. Goodness, the triplets had even taken to calling Carter "Papa C."

So when she'd received Carter's text

message about tonight, she had encouraged Autumn to head home.

She couldn't get what Autumn had said out of her head. *I've seen the way he looks at you.* Her words shouldn't have, but they'd given Emma a spark of hope she was still trying to extinguish.

Yet she was certain the hope would be snuffed out as soon as Carter arrived and told her whatever bleak story had made him disappear.

She stepped back and surveyed the table with a blooming lavender plant Esther had brought over as the centerpiece. Tomorrow, Emma would plant it next to the new family store for a pop of color. A glint out the kitchen window caught her attention. With Autumn's help, she'd strung lights around the family store porch. Every time she spotted the structure, she thought of Carter. And how he'd pushed her to reimagine the space. How he'd organized the town event to rebuild the family store. And how he'd added the wide covered porch for her early birthday gift. Her eyes filled with tears, but she looked away and focused on organizing the food for dinner instead of dwelling on the moment.

Noises emitted from her phone. The triplets were waking up. She needed to change her clothes and put on a little makeup before she got them up to play for a bit before Carter arrived.

Her stomach twirled at the thought of seeing Carter again. That was crazy because she had seen him every day for months on end and hadn't had this strong of an emotional response to him.

Maybe it was because he had been here that she hadn't even thought of him leaving.

She strode into her bedroom and slipped into the halter dress she'd picked out after Autumn had left earlier. A grim realization hit her. She had taken his presence for granted. While she curled her hair, she gritted her teeth at her thoughtless actions, not that letting him know how she felt would have changed a thing.

She opened the door to the triplets' room and they all looked up from their toddler beds. Addie and Cassie were leaning against Addie's headboard "reading" a book together. Mikey was flipped around on his bed, his feet leaning against the wall while he rubbed his eyes. Oh, how she loved her children and hoped Carter intended to remain in their lives. They needed him.

She herded them into the playroom and nervously paced while she waited for Carter to arrive.

When the doorbell rang, her nerves fluttered. How come he hadn't let himself in? Was he proving a point that he was now a guest here and would be an infrequent visitor? She prayed not.

She strode to the front door to let him in and what she saw stopped her cold.

Carter looked unsure of himself while he handed her a beautiful bouquet of fragrant red roses wrapped in cellophane and a red box of candy in the shape of a heart. Her pulse skittered at the meaning behind the gifts. Though they were cheesy, they weren't random objects that he'd purchased. Red roses and candy, especially chocolate in a red box the shape of a heart, usually meant one thing. Love. But she hadn't thought he cared for her in that way.

She gazed into his face and what she spotted made her pause. Maybe he hadn't left for good. Maybe there was still a possibility for them as a couple.

He appeared to have dressed up, crisp dress pants and an emerald-green polo shirt that brought out the warm undertones of his gorgeous chocolate eyes. His masculine scent tickled her senses.

Man, she had missed him.

"I'm sorry," he whispered as regret covered his face. The way his eyes drank her in gave her a hopeful expectation.

"Papa C," the children screamed as they rushed him. She must have left the baby gate open.

Carter crouched low and opened his arms. The children all landed on him at once and, at their weight, he toppled over onto the porch, laughing.

He lay splayed out, half on the porch and half inside the house, while the triplets flooded him with hugs and kisses. The radiant joy on Carter's face gave her hope.

But then she took a step back, concerned that maybe he was only here for dinner and then he'd vanish again.

She placed the candy and flowers on the little entry table and crossed her arms in front of her body as the little lovefest continued. Carter hadn't been around like usual for three days. Unless he had a convincing explanation for deserting them, her job was to protect the triplets.

She refused to allow her children to be a pawn in any game Carter was playing.

Carter couldn't stop grinning as he and the triplets scrambled to stand. How they called him Papa C tilted his heart. They each wanted to show him something in the playroom. Mikey, a new dump truck. Addie, some colorful blocks Miss Esther had given them. Cassie, a new baby doll that cried when her pacifier fell out. He let them drag him into the playroom, thrilled they didn't hate him for not being around as much the past few days.

He glanced at his gorgeous wife. She looked stunning in a floral sundress and her curled hair highlighted her tan shoulders.

But the frown on her face proved he had a lot of explaining to do. *Lord, give me the right words tonight.* He'd missed Emma. He was hopeful he'd be able to share his feelings with her, and that she'd understand.

He settled on the area carpet and the triplets crawled on him like monkeys, apparently forgetting all about the special toys they had wanted to share. Tears edged his lashes as he swallowed the thickness of emotion in his throat. Boy, he'd missed being with them every moment he wasn't working. He roughed up Mikey's hair, squeezed Addie back and opened the book Cassie had handed him. He'd read, play trains, push them on swings, anything as long as he could be with these children again every day.

"Twain?" Mikey scrambled back to grab two trains, holding one toward Carter.

Carter smiled. "Let's take turns. As soon as I finish reading Cassie's book, I'll come play trains with you. Okay, buddy?"

Mikey grinned and scooted next to Carter to join in on listening to him read. Carter's heart was full. But he wanted more. He glanced at Emma as she stood in the corner, arms hugging her waist.

The triplets were easy to win over. Emma, however, might be a challenge.

After dinner, with the triplets providing the entertainment so he couldn't guess at what Emma was thinking, she didn't shoo him away. Nerves swirled in his belly because as soon as the triplets were in bed, they'd talk.

At least she appeared open to hearing him out. A little while later, Carter followed Emma and closed the triplets' bedroom door.

"I've missed this tradition," he said.

She nodded, but her face was taut. No matter how much the rejection would hurt, it was time to lay it all out. Explain how he had fallen in love with her. And how he'd been fearful she'd never be able to love him back.

"I owe you an explanation," he stated while standing in the hallway. Ugh, why hadn't he waited until they were back in the playroom? He guessed part of him was afraid she was about to make him leave.

An abundance of emotions covered her face. First surprise then she pursed her lips as though upset, but then her features cleared and he might have seen hope. Yes, he'd cling to that, because what he had to tell her would be hard.

"Let's sit on the porch," she said.

His chest gave a tight squeeze at her words. She was getting him onto the porch to kick him out. He knew a dismissal when he heard it.

Sure, she'd told him she didn't want him moving back to his bungalow because people would talk. But maybe she was ready to let everyone know they hadn't married for love but for health insurance. Maybe she was about to tell him it had been refreshing not having him around these past few days and she no longer needed him here at night to monitor the herd since the dogs were trained.

Because, in reality, their marriage of convenience was only for Addie's medication. He'd gotten caught up in playing daddy and maybe by stepping away, she'd discovered she liked not having him around. As they walked toward the door, a knot tightened in his gut. Carter yearned for things to go back to the way they were before the workday so he could be a large part of the triplets' lives again. To remain on Jubilee Farm and help with the chores and be a part of everyday life here. Most of all, he ached for Emma to be his real wife.

As the front door clicked closed behind them, he stopped at what he saw. Twinkle lights decorated the front of the family store, including the covered porch he'd insisted she needed. His birthday gift for her. She must have liked the space to jazz it up like that.

"That looks so nice," he said. When had she set these lights up? He'd been in the RV working or pacing for three days and hadn't seen her out there once.

She crossed the gravel drive and he followed. Oh, she meant they could sit on the family store porch. Maybe that was a good thing considering how decorated and…romantic it was out here. His stomach flipped in little circles with a longing for this night to be the start of a glorious future for them.

The engagement ring he had purchased

with hope in his heart bumped against his leg with every step he took. They settled at the middle bistro table, awkwardness like a third person between them.

"I need to apologize for my disappearing act." He gulped away the nervous lump in his throat. "When the work was complete the other day, I came to show you the pictures, but you were asleep."

Her brows rose. "Really?" She licked her ruby lips.

"You were fitfully sleeping, so I turned to leave, but then you said Robbie's name. Twice."

Her lips formed a perfect *O* in surprise.

"It honestly scared me." He cleared his throat. "See, I have fallen in love with you. Right then, I knew you could never love me, so I did the only thing I could think of. I hid in the RV."

As he spoke, her eyes softened and her plump lips parted as though surprised he had such powerful feelings for her.

"But I'm back." He gave her a nod, letting her know he understood they had a business arrangement and he wouldn't push her. "I've missed being with you and the triplets. And if all we have is a forever friendship, I can survive. I'd rather have you as a friend than not have you in my life." There. That had been hard, but at least she knew.

She cleared her throat. "I have something to tell you."

He was afraid to look at her face for fear he'd see something like sympathy. This entire scene made him think of a Dear John letter. Was she about to break up with him? Had she realized, once he'd put distance between them, that things were better without him? *Dear Lord, please no. I can't live without Emma. She's the breath in my lungs.*

He chanced a look at her face and saw such a deep affection that hope ignited in his chest.

"I've fallen in love with you, too," she whispered. Her features showed apprehension and excitement. Clearly, she was unsure about how she felt about her new-found feelings.

He was shocked and thrilled at the same time. If ever he'd heard an opening to propose marriage, this was it.

He situated himself in a kneeling position in front of her, the engagement ring at the ready. His pulse hammered so hard in his ears that he was afraid she could hear it.

"Emma, I have fallen ever so deeply in love with you." Encouraged by the glistening tears in her eyes, he licked his dry lips, hoping they were tears of joy. "I admire how you manage the triplets with such grace and compassion, how this farm is a labor of love and that you allowed me into your life. But mostly I adore how selfless, brave and loyal you are." Her reaction was priceless. Her smile was genuine and huge, so he knew the tears streaming down her face were happy ones.

"Oh, Carter." She didn't seem to know what to say. But he did.

"I would be honored if you would become my real wife." In response, she threw her arms around him and squeezed.

"Yes, yes, yes!"

He stood and twirled her around, the twinkle lights sparkling in celebration of their engagement. Even though he had been fearful of getting hurt again, he thanked God for giving him the idea and courage to marry Emma so she and the triplets could be on his insurance plan. Not only did he have a wife to love, who loved him back, but he had adorable triplets to help raise.

"The children are going to be so happy," Emma stated.

"I adore Mikey, Cassie and Addie." He was thankful God had helped him traverse the instant family situation. Why had he been so worried about keeping up with the triplets when what children wanted the most was love and support, not a playful friend? They needed parents to be there for them, which Carter was able and thrilled to do.

"And they adore you." She gave a little satisfied sigh that made his heart race with delight.

Emma inhaled Carter's comforting scent, feeling woozy by his proclamation and proposal. She squeezed his neck a little tighter, not wanting to let go. Her insides had ripped apart from hearing what he'd gone through in her fever-induced sleep. Yes, she loved Robbie and would never forget him, but he'd be happy that she was able to open her heart to Carter, thrilled the triplets would have a new dad and that she would have a helpmate for life.

The moon combined with the twinkle lights to cast a silvery glow over Jubilee Farm and the family store porch. Her pulse sped when she spotted excitement and a bit of disbelief on Carter's features. She felt the same.

"I love you," she whispered, amazed they were in this romantic setting. Engaged!

Only God could have arranged her desperate need for medical insurance to coincide with Carter's ingenious idea of marrying. Because if she hadn't been forced into close proximity with him, she never would have let her guard down and fallen in love. She hadn't realized how tightly she'd been holding on to Robbie's memory and how unhealthy that was for a young woman and her children.

"The ring," Carter exclaimed. He opened the velvet box. Nestled within was a gorgeous square diamond set between two sets of three smaller diamonds. This must have cost a fortune, but she held her tongue, trying to learn from her past mistakes. It was exquisite.

She caught her lower lip between her teeth as he pulled it out of the box and slid it onto her finger. She lifted it to the light. It sparkled brightly under the twinkle lights. "It's gorgeous."

"You're gorgeous," he whispered.

She looked into his smoldering eyes and she trembled at what the future held with him. Gently, he framed her face with his hands, lowered his head and pressed his lips against hers, capturing every stray thought inside her head. She looped her arms around his neck, sinking into the kiss. The affection between them was powerful because it had been building for over a month now. She melted into the kiss, wishing it could last forever.

She knew Carter would never walk away again. They'd both make mistakes, but as long as they talked, they'd work things out.

When they parted, her pulse raced at their first kiss, with hope for many more to come. She would show him every day how much she adored him. And how grateful she was that he was her husband.

He leaned back and gazed into her twinkling eyes. "I love you, Mrs. McCaw, more than you could ever imagine."

She grinned, thrilled at the work God had done in both of their lives but ready to start living life with Carter. "How about a short engagement?"

"I was thinking the same thing." His excited eyes sparkled at their future. "But your ceremony with Robbie was also at a courthouse and I'd like our vow renewal to be a special memory for both you and the triplets. Maybe we could celebrate at Laney's wedding venue?"

Her chest constricted at his thoughtfulness, but she didn't want to wait too long. She pursed her lips and he gave her a quick kiss.

"I'm confident Laney can throw a small wedding together quickly. Hopefully, in a couple of weeks?"

Her heart was full. Overfull, really.

She had dreamed of having a real marriage with Carter for weeks now. Of him moving into the house with her and the triplets. The family store fire had allowed her to release Robbie from her heart and fully fall in love with her handsome husband.

God had provided and then some.

Epilogue

On Thanksgiving, Emma closed the truck door and breathed in the crisp coolness of the November day. Across the truck hood, she gazed at her grinning husband, who gave her a knowing wink. Butterflies took flight in her belly at his attention.

She opened the rear door with a giant bowl of her famous mousse balanced on her left palm. Cassie and Addie scrambled out without a care in the world. In the past month, the three of them had learned to unbuckle themselves from their forward-facing car seats. Emma had been concerned about their safety, but Carter had recommended implementing a safety plan: if one of them unbuckled while the car was running, they lost all television privileges for the next day. Since the triplets didn't get to watch much television, they all valued the privilege and didn't want to lose it. Emma was all for the plan and was thankful for a partner in parenting.

Along with Carter and Mikey, she and the girls brushed their way through colorful fall leaves scattered on the ground toward Cora and Wade's front porch.

"Maybe we can rake the leaves into a pile and you guys can jump in them," Carter said. In response, the triplets surrounded their father screaming, *"Please."* A satisfied smile perched on his lips and a prideful gleam glistened in his eyes. If she hadn't had a medical insurance crisis six months ago, she and Carter would not be experiencing the joys of a newlywed life or parenting together or running Jubilee Farm together. God was so good. He had met them where they were and gently moved them into the future neither of them ever thought possible.

As Emma mounted the steps, the triplets spotted a tiny pile of leaves and rushed over to jump in them, screaming in delight even though they only came up to their three-year-old knees. She placed the heavy mousse on a little table to wait for the children. Carter stepped beside her and slipped his hand in hers.

She looked up into his adoring face and couldn't believe she'd been given a second chance at love. Two true loves in one lifetime. That could only be from God.

While the children were stomping on the leaves, Carter tugged her to him and pressed his lips against hers. She melted into his arms.

A throat-clearing interrupted their moment. With her arms still wrapped around her husband's neck, she eyed the now-open front door with Autumn, palm supporting her swollen belly, standing there.

"You guys are late," Autumn stated, laughter dancing in her eyes.

"When you have three-year-old triplets to get ready and corral into a truck when all they want to do is play with humongous dogs, then you can judge," Carter joked as he brushed past his sister, his hand securely holding Emma's while the triplets scrambled up the steps and rushed past them to play with their cousins in the old dining room, now the grandchildren's playroom.

"I guess I'll get the mousse," Autumn called out.

Emma smiled. She just loved how his siblings interacted with one another—with love and respect and always a touch of humor.

As they made their way through the house, he rubbed the back of her hand with his thumb, sending a warm sensation up her arm and settling into her core. She glanced at their children, all happily playing with the fresh toys and their many cousins.

"Look, the newlyweds are finally here," Wyatt teased from the other side of the play area.

Emma felt her cheeks heat at the ribbing.

Wyatt crossed the room and gave Carter a quick side hug with a pat on the shoulder. He asked how the dogs were doing guarding their flock. Because she missed their contact, Emma placed a hand on her husband's upper arm.

"Look at you." Wyatt slapped his arm. "You never thought you'd have a wife or children or be a rancher, and yet now you have all three." The brothers exchanged a look that made her chest fluttery at how her husband's life had changed since they'd married. "Of course, your farm is full of small livestock, not cattle, so I'm not sure if you really qualify for the title of rancher. I think you're more like a farmer."

They chuckled at her brother-in-law's definition of rancher, but even though

Wyatt was half joking, Carter seemed to stand a little taller now that his brother had given him an official farmer title. Goat farmer. She liked it.

"Autumn and I have the children. If you want, you can join the others."

She shared a contented look with Carter as they headed to the hub of the home—the kitchen—with his strong hand in hers. After their wedding vow renewal, he'd told her that he believed hands were meant to be held. Since then, he'd kept to that belief. When they were together, they were always connected, either by holding hands, or hugging, or his arm draped over her shoulders. She adored the constant affection.

Tangy stuffing and the candied smell of sweet potato casserole filled her senses as they stepped into the bustling kitchen. She'd never had a Thanksgiving celebration like this. Tears misted her eyes at the sight, knowing this was her present and future. She was thankful her children would only have memories like today. She tipped her head against Carter's shoulder. "I love you," she whispered.

When she saw him eyeing Ethan carving the turkey, she pushed him in that direction and moved to the island to help. To her left was the finally finished recent addition to her in-law's home, a swanky new dining room to accommodate their growing family. The custom table was about the length of the one she'd heard about at the Biltmore Estate in North Carolina. She clapped a hand to her chest when she spotted the myriad of pretty place settings. "Oh, Cora, the table is beautiful. And those fall-colored flowers are so festive." She had much to learn about raising a family and creating a hospitable home from Carter's mother. And she couldn't wait.

Cora turned and wiped her hands on a dishtowel. "Willow sent me a picture for the inspiration, aren't they pretty?" A touch of sadness covered her face as she spoke of the daughter-in-law she hadn't seen in a while. Willow was Owen McCaw's wife. From what Emma had gathered, there was some type of rift with Owen and his parents, since he rarely visited from his home in North Carolina. But maybe she was guessing wrong.

Cora engulfed Emma in a welcoming hug that screamed, *You are family*. Tears streamed down Emma's face. She again thanked God for His provision. "Emma, it's so good to have you here." Cora leaned back and gripped her shoulders. "And to have Carter at peace."

Emma swiped at her eyes, unsure of what to say. But before she could speak, Laney asked Cora to check the thickness of the gravy, so her mother-in-law turned around.

Emma had never allowed herself to dream. As an orphan, she'd simply survived. When she'd married an orphan, it had made sense that they'd create their own traditions within their family of five.

But now. Now she had all this. The dream she never knew she had was now a reality.

All because Addie had needed a special medication covered by insurance that Emma didn't have.

Carter moved beside her and slid his sturdy arm across her shoulders. "What are you thinking about?"

"I'm happier than I ever thought I could be."

"God is good, isn't He?"

He sure was.

* * * * *

Dear Reader,

Thank you for joining me on Emma and Carter's journey in Serenity, Texas, the fourth installment of the Triple C Ranch series. I loved writing this sweet love story.

I'm a sucker for a romance, but when it comes to marriage of convenience, I need a Biblical scenario that I can get behind. So, in this story, we see a man who has no plans of ever marrying thrown together with a woman who has lost the love of her life. They are both devoted to God and enter their marriage of convenience, each committed to a lifetime of marriage with the other, which makes it even sweeter when they discover they are in love! I hope you enjoyed reading Emma and Carter's story.

It would be fantastic to connect with you. Drop me a note at heidimain.com. While there, you can sign up for my newsletter for book news, giveaways and life reports.

Hugs,
Heidi